'e won't win,' Bernadette said. 'Chiquita's so lazy and I'm ly good at sport and maths, and I don't think you're very od at anything except getting in trouble.'

I nearly told Bernadette that she wasn't good at anything cept being grumpy but I decided to ignore her and let r go to sleep.

There must be something we could do. I would test s in all possible areas of talent and find out something amazing we could do. Something that would win the talent contest and make us the star of the Christmas show so hat we had to be in the documentary and, therefore, make anielle so upset and enraged she'd think the night she was overed in rotten eggs was the best night of her life.

Also available by Annie Caulfield:

KATIE MILK SOLVES CRIMES and so on . . .

KATIE MILK

solves
REALITY-TV CRIMES

annie caulfield

CORGI YEARLING BOOKS

KATIE MILK SOLVES REALITY-TV CRIMES
A CORGI YEARLING BOOK 978 0 440 86687 9

Published in Great Britain by Corgi Yearling,
an imprint of Random House Children's Books

This edition published 2007

1 3 5 7 9 10 8 6 4 2

Copyright © Annie Caulfield, 2007

Papers used by Random House Children's Books are natural,
recyclable products made from wood grown in sustainable forests.
The manufacturing processes conform to the environmental
regulations of the country of origin.

Set in 12/16pt Janson by
Falcon Oast Graphic Art Ltd.

Corgi Yearling Books are published by
Random House Children's Books,
61–63 Uxbridge Road, London W5 5SA,
a division of The Random House Group Ltd,
Addresses for companies within The Random House Group can be found at
www.randomhouse.co.uk

THE RANDOM HOUSE GROUP Limited Reg. No. 954009
www.**kids**at**random**house.co.uk

A CIP catalogue record for this book is available from the British Library.

Printed and bound in Great Britain by
CPI Antony Rowe, Eastbourne

For Jasmine Mary Jude Warwick.
One all to yourself this time,
with lots of love

CHAPTER ONE

'Waaah! Yuuuk! Arrrgh! Waaaaah!'

It's a bit hard to write down, but you get the idea – someone was screaming their head off. Even better, it was Danielle who was screaming her head off and we could hear her all the way down the corridor in our bedroom.

By the way, in case you're wondering who 'we' are, it's me, Katie Milk, and my friends, Bernadette and Chiquita, and we were pleased to hear Danielle screaming. It meant she must have slid down slap bang into the middle of the eggs we'd put in her bed. Ten eggs. Slimy and disgusting with bits of scratchy shell and so on.

It was also *bad* that Danielle was screaming, because it was only a matter of time before a nun came and asked who'd put eggs in her bed. By the way, in case you didn't know, a nun is a religious woman who teaches and looks after people in some kinds of old-fashioned boarding schools. I just thought I'd tell you that in case you'd never heard of such a thing, or been to a boarding school with nuns such as this one me and my friends had been sent to . . . Anyway, as far as the screams of Danielle attracting nuns were concerned, we had worked out that this would happen and decided it would be worth it. Danielle would scream; nuns would come. We'd have to own up and be punished. We'd have to own up because this was a school where, if anything bad happened, the nuns would just go on and on until someone owned up, even for really small crimes like talking in class, let alone big eggs-in-the-bed type crimes.

Oh, and these were eggs that had gone bad, just to make it an even more disgusting type crime.

But, as I said, we'd decided that horrifying Danielle to the point of screaming was worth any punishment that might happen to us afterwards. If you knew Danielle, I absolutely promise you that you'd agree with me on this. And if you'd been me, you'd also have swiped any bad eggs you came across to use on Danielle.

I'd got the opportunity when I was helping with the washing-up in the kitchen as a punishment for passing notes to my friend Chiquita in class. I'd heard the old nuns who worked in the kitchen talking while they were making a cake. One made 'Yeuch' noises when she cracked a couple of eggs and realized that the whole tray was probably off. The other one said they should take the tray of eggs back to the farm and complain. The first one said it was their own fault – they'd left them too close to the radiator.

Meanwhile the smell of the bad egg was wafting over to my side of the kitchen – a mix of toilets and old fireworks. Yeuch.

The nun with the radiator opinion won: the eggs were to be binned. So I said in my kindest, most-helpful-to-nuns voice, 'I'll put them out in the bins for you, Sisters.'

And they said, 'Oh, thank you, darling, what a good child you are . . .' And so on.

I grabbed an old carrier bag from behind the kitchen door as I went out to the bins, and carefully tipped the eggs into the bag. Then I took off my cardigan and folded it around the carrier bag, so hopefully the nuns would just think I'd got hot doing strenuous bin activity.

They weren't really looking when I left the kitchen because they were busy filling up the salt pots. They liked this job for some reason and always concentrated hard not to spill any, saying things like: 'Hold the funnel steady now, Sister. Your hand's shaking . . . It *is* shaking, Sister, I'm telling you, it's shaking . . .' And giggling like this was all hilarious.

I found my friends Chiquita and Bernadette and showed them the treasure I'd rescued from the bins. We crept upstairs before evening study and spread the stinking eggs inside Danielle's bed. It was a messy job, with lots of retching involved, and several hand-washings afterwards to get rid of the smell.

But now we were hearing the fantastic results of all that

hard work. Danielle was whining on and on at the top of her voice.

'Oh, it's so disgusting, I'm covered in egg – it stinks. I'm going to vomit . . . Oh, Sister, it's disgusting . . .'

Danielle was saying 'Sister' to Sister Ita, the nun who looked after the bedrooms. She had obviously arrived at the scene of the crime annoyingly soon.

Sister Ita had a red face like a round balloon. But her head wasn't filled with air. She guessed things quickly. Instead of calling all the girls together, she immediately charged down the corridor to our room. She knew we didn't like Danielle and that made us her number-one suspects.

Even before we were accused of egg crimes, we were already in trouble because Chiquita was out of her own bedroom and in talking to me and my roommate, Bernadette. But we'd sort of decided we should all be together to be punished, seeing as we'd committed the crime together.

Don't go thinking we were bad people for this. Danielle might be very beautiful, with a long blonde plait and a sweet Scottish accent. She might laugh cheerfully all the time and be good at everything – but underneath she was the meanest goat-faced pig you could ever meet in your life.

For instance, since we'd all come back from half-term, she'd gone on about how Bernadette, who'd had an illness and had to have an operation to stop her smelling of wee, still smelled of wee a bit. This was *simply not true*. Then she said to everyone that I only had a mum and no dad, because my mum didn't have a husband ever, and had so many boyfriends she couldn't tell who my real dad was anyway. This was *simply not true*. And Danielle said that Chiquita, whose mum was a famous supermodel, didn't look like her stunningly beautiful mum at all. This was *not exactly true*. Chiquita was quite pretty, though in an ordinary-person sort of way – but if everyone looked like stunningly beautiful models, what would be the point of models? And you could see by Chiquita's big eyes and lovely long black hair that Stella Diaz, supermodel, was her mum. You just couldn't see it right away.

Anyway, Danielle deserved egging for telling all those spiteful lies. She also deserved egging for getting herself popular throughout the whole school with what me, Bernadette and Chiquita agreed was cheap and pathetic blackmail.

Danielle had four older brothers. Toby, the oldest, was a television producer and director. She showed off about this a lot. And now Toby was going to make a reality-TV programme at our school. This was a bit weird because normally we weren't even allowed to *watch* TV at our school. There'd just be a DVD of some ancient and usually childish film on Saturday night. But the nuns had been bribed. Toby's television company was giving them some money to send to their nun friends who worked with lepers and sick people in India.

During half-term all our parents had signed a letter to say they agreed to the filming. Even though, horrifically, my mum had started going on about how she thought the documentary was a bad idea, and there was too much reality TV frying people's minds into mush and silliness, and if the television people cared so much about lepers, why didn't they just give the nuns the money for free . . .? I had to beg and pretend to cry so she signed the letter. Otherwise I might have been the only person in the school who had no chance of being on television and Danielle would have just loved that.

Danielle, obviously, would be the star of the documentary, because her brother was making it. She'd gained a ton of popularity by hinting that people who were her friends could be in the documentary a lot too. And people like me, Bernadette and Chiquita, who she hated, would hardly be in it at all.

Bernadette kept saying things to Danielle like, 'Who cares about being in some boring "life at a boarding school" documentary?'

And I'd say the same kind of things. Although I did care. But I wasn't going to let Danielle know. Also, I figured that I would soon think up some spectacular and heroic actions to be doing, so the crew would have to film me. And obviously they'd have to film Chiquita because of her having a famous mum. So only Bernadette would be left out – and she really, honestly seemed not to care about being on TV. But Bernadette was extremely strange.

Although Bernadette could make up great stories and be very funny, she was mostly bad-tempered. As I mentioned, when I first came to the school, she'd had an illness that made her smell of wee all the time. It was a bad illness in lots of ways, but obviously the smelling-of-wee part was the worst for Bernadette. It meant that she was horrible to people first, before they could be horrible to her. And even now that she'd had an operation and been cured of her illness – and smell – she'd kept her bad temper. And her habit of deliberately not liking anything other people liked, just to be difficult.

If everyone wanted to be on television, it was typical of Bernadette to say she didn't care a scrap about television. Which was a shame. Bernadette was good at sport and most lessons. She deserved to be the star of any film about the school far more than Danielle. But it looked as though Danielle was going to be filmed, be famous and be totally unbearable.

It was a shame that the television people weren't around to film Danielle in her fancy silk pyjamas covered in rotten eggs. It was a shame we couldn't see through walls to find out what she looked like in the eggs. It was a shame that red-faced Sister Ita was in our room saying, 'Was it you three who put eggs in Danielle's bed – and, Chiquita, why are you in this room anyway?'

Now, personally, I would have not owned up. Because I didn't think eggs were a serious thing, and anyway, Danielle deserved it. But I knew Bernadette would own up because she had been at this posh school since she was seven and they'd made her believe you absolutely always had to own up or you'd be as bad as the devil. Whereas I'd only been at the school for half a term and had previously gone to the sort of school where people laughed at you for owning up and no one owned up even if ten policemen ran all around the place asking questions with dogs.

Owning up or not owning up didn't matter anyway, because Chiquita looked at Sister Ita and said, 'How did you know it was us?'

I liked Chiquita for lots of reasons, but she could be a bit dim.

'I knew it was you because I just knew,' Sister Ita said. 'Now go to your room, Chiquita, because all three of you will be getting up an hour early to help in the kitchen. And you'll be helping in the kitchen every morning and every break time for a week.' Sister Ita stared at us, then seemed to decide her punishment wasn't enough. 'And the three of you can stand up at assembly in the morning and make a public apology to Danielle.'

Without thinking, I let out a groan.

'You groan away, Katherine, but you're still going to

apologize. Come on now, Chiquita, out of here.'

She went out, shooing Chiquita in front of her.

Bernadette threw herself back on her bed with a big sigh. 'I hate this school,' she said.

'We should have thought about the eggs more,' I said. 'Thought of a way to make it look like someone else did it, or burglars did it or something.'

'Who cares?' Bernadette said. 'We'd probably have got blamed even if we hadn't done it.'

Because Bernadette was like that – if there was a bad side of things to imagine, she'd imagine it.

So those were my friends: Bernadette the Miserable, who didn't smell of wee, although she used to; and Chiquita, a bit dim, who had a supermodel mum.

Oh, and just after lights-out, the door banged open and my not-friend, Danielle, barged into the room.

CHAPTER TWO

Danielle whispered, really furious: 'Sister Ita says you have to apologize to me at assembly but I don't care about that. I'm here to tell you that none of you three will be in Toby's documentary, not even for a second. And I'll be the star of it and be famous.'

'Get lost,' Bernadette said.

'Oh, very intelligent argument,' Danielle said, and flounced off.

Bernadette made a growling sound. 'It's so pathetic that she thinks it's important to be on TV.'

'Pathetic,' I agreed.

I couldn't say to Bernadette that I was actually really upset about not being on television. She would think that was worse than pathetic. But I had lots of reasons to want to be famous and on television. One of them had actually been caused by Danielle. She kept on saying I had no proper dad. But I *did* have one; he'd run off not long after my mum married him, before I was even born. So he wouldn't recognize me. But possibly, if I was famous on television and in magazines, I could say in interviews about my run-off dad and he'd realize it was him. From clues like my age and where I came from, he'd work it out. Then he'd feel ashamed and come looking for me.

Once that had happened, Danielle couldn't keep telling her disgusting lies about my mum having too many boyfriends and so on.

Also, there was being rich. If I was rich and famous then my mum wouldn't have to work lots of shifts as a nurse. It was all very well that we'd had a weird inheritance from my Auntie Apricot to pay for me to go to this posh school, but there was no actual money for us until I was eighteen, and that was on the condition that I stayed at the nuns' school until then. And, believe me, although I had friends, there were days when it was just so horrible at the nuns' school that I'd have loved to find another way to get some money.

Also – and I think this is just normal – being the centre of attention and fussed over by everybody would surely be a cool way to live. Maybe Bernadette was right; it was pathetic to want things like tons of money and attention. But how would I know she was right until I'd tried it?

I wasn't alone. Chiquita had a famous mum but she said she wanted to show everyone she could do famous things on her own. She really wanted to be interesting for her own sake, but she couldn't think of anything she was good at. She'd confessed to me that secretly she would love to be doing something in the documentary, but now, it seemed, it wouldn't happen, so she might as well forget it.

I had to work out how I could make sure we were in the reality-TV show without Bernadette thinking I'd made plans and schemes to get us in it. Not that me and Chiquita were scared of her or anything; we just hated being called 'pathetic'. Especially as, maybe, in our hearts, we knew it *was* all a bit pathetic.

Then I had a brilliant idea and had to annoy Bernadette by speaking to her when she'd nearly fallen asleep.

'You know, Bernadette, if we somehow manage to be in the documentary, Danielle will be furious.'

She made a grunting sound.

Then I had a second amazing idea.

'Listen – she can't keep us out of the programme if we win the talent contest.'

'What?' Bernadette murmured grumpily.

I knew I was right. The whole reason for making the documentary just now was to film the talent contest that was held every autumn to decide which girls would be in the Christmas show for parents. And if we won our class talent contest . . .

'We won't win,' Bernadette said. 'Chiquita's so lazy and I'm only good at sport and maths, and I don't think you're very good at anything except getting in trouble.'

I nearly told Bernadette that she wasn't good at anything

except being grumpy but I decided to ignore her and let her go to sleep.

There must be something we could do. I would test us in all possible areas of talent and find out something amazing we could do. Something that would win the talent contest and make us the star of the Christmas show so that we had to be in the documentary and, therefore, make Danielle so upset and enraged she'd think the night she was covered in rotten eggs was the best night of her life.

CHAPTER THREE

I didn't like getting up at six o'clock to work in the kitchen. The whole place smelled of weird chemicals from the big dishwasher that we had to load and unload, as well as washing pots, setting the tables for breakfast and general other boring stuff – but I wasn't crying about it like Chiquita. Chiquita did tend to cry about everything. Although in this instance it was useful because the nuns who worked in the kitchen felt so sorry for her they gave her chocolate biscuits, then had to give some to me and Bernadette so we weren't left out.

Everyone called the nuns who did the cooking and washing up 'the kitchen nuns', but their real names were Sister Finton and Sister Legori. They were both Irish, both old, and both very tiny and hunched over. Also they both had quite hairy faces. Possibly Sister Legori was the most hairy. In fact, you might even think she was wearing a little stick-on beard. Except it was all her own beard. Which was impressive.

Sister Finton and Sister Legori had very red hands, all gnarled up as if they'd been made wrong. Their feet had bumps sticking out of the sides and back that they said were their 'bunions'. They had to wear specially misshapen shoes to fit them. If you thought about their feet too much, you might get repulsed, but the kitchen nuns were sweet, in a gobliny sort of way, always whispering and giggling and giving you treats if you worked in the kitchen.

I had the feeling they were bossed around a lot by the other nuns and to get their revenge they cooked really terrible food. They made stews full of fatty lumps, pies that were nearly all grey pastry, grey scrambled eggs; even their baked beans seemed to have been watered down with some grey dye added. Sometimes our food had strange things turning up in it: plastic lids, metal screws and – worst of all – bits of hair that Bernadette said came from the beards. I just ate bread and butter or fruit most of the time, because the kitchen nuns couldn't get at those.

Strangely, though, in the kitchen they had boxes of nice biscuits, cakes and sweets that seemed to be just for themselves or their helpers. Biscuits, cakes and sweets from shops, without lids, screws or beard bits.

They always called us 'my darlings' or 'darling wee children', and they had an old dog called Tara that slept under the kitchen table. Tara was a brown, smelly, hairy dog of no particular kind, but you could see that Sister Finton and Sister Legori loved him. They were always giving him things to eat and talking to him, telling him what was going on.

'Now, Tara, this is Bernadette, Chiquita and Katie here to help us this morning,' Sister Finton said. Then she looked at me. 'You see, darling, poor Tara's nearly blind so we have to tell him who's here or he feels left out.'

Bernadette said what I was thinking: 'It's a he? But isn't Tara a girl's name?'

The little nuns laughed. 'Oh, silly child, Tara is a place in Ireland. We named him after the place, not the girl's name.'

Sister Legori got so giggly that she had a coughing fit. 'They think we gave a boy dog a girl's name. If we'd done that, we'd be very strange indeed, wouldn't we, Sister Finton?'

'Yes, we would indeed, Sister,' Sister Finton said, patting the other nun on the back to stop her coughing fit. Then Sister Finton started giggling and coughing too, so they had to sit down and drink glasses of water until they were normal again. Although, as you can tell, possibly they were not quite normal even when they were normal.

A bit later on, when we'd set the tables, Sister Legori said, 'What lovely good children you are – we've everything done before time. You can go out into the back yard and play with Tara till breakfast.'

Being very old and nearly blind, Tara wasn't a great dog to play with. If you threw his rubber ball, he would walk slowly across the yard and pick it up. Then he'd walk really slowly back and put it at your feet, really, really slowly. Not exactly exciting.

But Tara could sit up and beg if you said, 'Sit up, Tara, darling,' in an Irish accent. So we did this for ages because it made us laugh doing the accent.

Soon, even though we'd been laughing a lot, we got a bit bored being with Tara in the yard. There was nothing much there: a concrete area with some dustbins, a big square patch of grass, a blue painted kennel for Tara, a sandpit for Tara's business – all surrounded with a high wooden fence and a gate with a big bolt.

The kitchen nuns had said to us: 'Whatever you do, children, don't open that gate or Tara will be off like a rocket, like a rocket to the moon! He's very nosy and loves a chance to get out in the countryside. Last time he got out he was gone for three days!'

We were a bit tempted to open the gate to see if Tara possibly could move like a rocket, but then if it was true and Tara got out . . . The thing is, the kitchen nuns were so cute and gobliny, it would have been very sad to see them upset. So we left the gate closed and kept playing 'sit up and beg', or waiting for Tara to slowly, slowly wander across the yard to fetch the ball and slowly, slowly creak his way back to whoever had thrown it.

As the dog games weren't too fascinating, I decided to try to talk about my talent-contest plan again.

'I can't do anything,' Chiquita said right away.

'And I can't and you can't,' Bernadette said.

'I can do stuff,' I said, annoyed at all this immediate negativity.

Bernadette looked at me with her little eyes and said, 'Like?'

My brain whirled round like a computer, desperately scrolling for stuff I could do. A dumb answer popped out: 'Detective stuff,' I said.

'Listen,' Bernadette said. 'You can't get up on stage and say, "OK, everybody, my act is . . . solving crimes." What are you going to do? A crime-solving dance? Juggle some crimes? Walk on stilts made of crimes . . . ?'

'All right, all right,' I said. Bernadette could be such a know-all sometimes. 'But I bet if we all really tried, we could find something to do.'

'If we all really tried, we could forget about the stupid talent contest and stupid Christmas show and stupid reality-TV programme,' Bernadette said.

'I agree with Bernadette. It's hopeless,' Chiquita said, because sometimes she was too lazy even to have her own ideas.

'But, Chiquita, you want to be in the documentary,' I argued. 'And the talent contest is our best chance.'

She made a pouty face and shrugged. 'No point. Danielle is fantastic at singing and dancing and everything, so she always wins.'

I couldn't believe how negative they were. But then I couldn't think of anything like singing or dancing, or even doing stuff on stilts, that I could possibly be good at.

At moments like this I didn't like being at boarding school and wanted to be back in north London with my mum, and at a normal school where people's brothers didn't have anything to do with television – except maybe being mentioned on *Crimewatch*.

The whole situation had made me depressed so I didn't say any more about the contest. I'd caught negativity from them and felt doomed.

We went back to playing ball with Tara until Sister Finton came out, telling us to wash our hands and join the other girls outside the dining room, where they were queuing up, waiting for breakfast.

Danielle was there with her roommate, Indira, the princess from India. She turned her head away and whispered to Indira as if she couldn't care less about us. Then suddenly she said loudly, 'Oh, what's that stink? It smells like some people must have been working in the kitchen.'

'That's where you're wrong,' Bernadette said. Bernadette had a skinny pointy face – when she got cross it seemed to get even pointier. 'We've been mucking around in the back garden – not working, just mucking around having a good time and playing with the dog.'

This wasn't a very smart 'so there' thing to say, but I

suppose it was better than nothing, which is all I could think of.

'Oh, not the nuns' disgusting dog.' Danielle laughed, looking round to check everyone was listening. 'I've got five great dogs at home. I wouldn't even count that monstrosity as a dog. And that's yet another thing that must be making you stink, apart from the usual wee smell.'

Some people who wanted to keep in with Danielle sniggered.

Indira just gave a slight smile, because she was stuck with Danielle as a roommate whether she liked her or not. And I'd been having a sneaking suspicion from this kind of slight-smiling-instead-of-laughing clue that Indira secretly didn't like Danielle.

'Better to stink than be totally stupid,' Bernadette said to Danielle as she stomped to the back of the queue, me and Chiquita following.

'Oh, sticks and stones,' Danielle said, which was such an annoying thing to say but it made all her fans giggle as if it was hilarious.

At the back of the queue Bernadette whispered furiously to me and Chiquita: 'Right, even if we have to commit terrible crimes to do it, we're winning that talent contest!'

CHAPTER FOUR

At morning assembly there was some praying, some hymn singing, and then Sister Vincent, the headmistress, stood up with a clipboard. This is when she read out any important announcements. Or talked about people who'd got into big trouble.

Sister Vincent was about six foot tall, with a mega-loud, booming voice. She taught sport things mostly and was supposed to be some sort of doctor in case any of us got sick. Everyone said that her idea of being a doctor was to give people aspirin – even if one of your legs fell off, she'd only give you an aspirin.

Although all the nuns were weird, Sister Vincent was one of the weirdest. In fact, I quite liked watching to see what weird thing she'd do or say next. She wore trainers with her nun's outfit to play sports and had a special 'action' veil for sports that was held on with a piece of elastic under her chin. She forgot people's names and sometimes forgot her own. When she spoke, she roared as if she was shouting over traffic in a tunnel, and she did talk a lot, usually about what was wrong with the modern world today. But she had a face like a kind horse and although she was always noisily fussing about things, it was hard to feel scared of her.

This morning was the first time since half-term that I'd seen her stand up with her clipboard looking cross. Her voice boomed across the hall: 'Sister Ita tells me there are girls in this school who think putting eggs in another girl's bed is a laughing matter.'

There was a titter of laughter all around the assembly hall.

'*This is no laughing matter!*' Sister Vincent bellowed so loudly that the windows shook and everyone made snurfling noises trying not to laugh any more.

'Firstly' – her huge voice drowned out the last of the laughter noises – 'firstly, there is the deplorable waste of eggs when there are people in the world starving.'

Sister Vincent was obsessed with starving people. She used to work in India so she was particularly always talking about how people were starving in India.

'Imagine my horror, to hear of such a thing. A whole *tray* of eggs wasted! Thoughtlessly wasted!'

She was shouting wildly now. But she didn't point out that it was rotten eggs we'd wasted. Would a starving person want rotten eggs? Imagine it: you're really starving and you get an egg that's off and stinking – wouldn't you hate that?

Not that I was going to start saying any of these arguments in the middle of assembly. Especially not when Sister Vincent was ranting on and on so insanely.

I looked over at Danielle. She was making a smug face like a holy saint. Indira was looking annoyed. I suppose if you were from India and actually a rich princess, you didn't like people saying there was nothing to India but starving-ness. It was like the way the headmistress before Sister Vincent had told me I was 'underprivileged' – that is, poor – and therefore bound to be always in trouble my whole life. You could be poor and not always in trouble and Indian and not starving. But nuns seemed to get very stuck in their ideas about people.

Sister Vincent suddenly stopped with the speech about starving people and said in a cold, slightly quieter voice, 'Katherine Milne, Chiquita Diaz and Bernadette Kelly, you three girls are to come up here beside me now and face the whole school in your shame.'

I wasn't exactly in shame but it was pretty embarrassing.

Chiquita started crying, of course, and Bernadette scowled, looking like she wanted to bite everybody.

When we were standing beside her, Sister Vincent glared at us, then turned to face the school. 'Secondly . . .' she announced.

Well, good, at least she was going to change from the starving-people subject . . .

'Secondly, you three disgraceful, wasteful little girls,

there is the issue of laundry. Sister Finton and Sister Legori have to do all the laundry as well as all the cooking, and you three silly, thoughtless little girls have pointlessly created extra laundry! I want no thoughtless laundry creation in this school, is that clear?'

Imagine the Queen of England really cross and yelling – that's what Sister Vincent sounded like. I was a bit sorry about making extra work for the kitchen nuns – I hadn't thought about that happening. But then maybe it was also the other important nuns' fault for making Sister Finton and Sister Legori do absolutely all the work.

Everyone in assembly shuffled around a bit, trying not to smile at each other about the way Sister Vincent was carrying on.

Sister Vincent turned to look at us thoughtless etceteras again. 'Now, Sister Ita has asked that you apologize publicly to Danielle Kirkham-Byles, as well as helping in the kitchen for this week, but I will tell you thoughtless, wasteful little girls something else. If there is one more episode of misbehaviour, you will be banned, completely banned, from competing in the talent contest for the Christmas concert.'

That made me feel very tense. It was so hard not to misbehave in this school. I got even more tense when Danielle was called forward to be apologized to. She looked like an extra smug, double holy saint.

'Sorry, Danielle.' Each one of us three thoughtless, wasteful and so on little girls apologized to her.

When we'd finished, she nodded. 'I accept your apologies. Thank you.'

If I'd had any more bad eggs, I'd have shoved one in her mouth. But that probably wouldn't have been a good way to stay in the talent contest.

'Very good, Danielle.' Sister Vincent smiled at her. 'That's very gracious of you.'

Sister Vincent liked Danielle. We'd have to be very careful about taking any other revenges on her. Danielle was captain of every sports team and lead singer in the choir – all Sister Vincent's pet areas. We'd have to be very, very careful indeed.

'Now,' Sister Vincent said. 'Girls wishing to take part in the talent contest for the Christmas show must put their names on the lists for each class outside the dining room by tomorrow night. I want you to put down your names and the act you're planning to do, so I can see the entrants have properly thought through what they'll be doing. By tomorrow night, seven o'clock.'

We had to think of an act. But what? And when would we get a chance to practise if we were working in the kitchen all week?

We had to make the best of things. When we'd finished washing up after lunch, we went out into the garden to play 'throwing the ball for Tara the dog' because we weren't allowed to leave the kitchen area even though we were finished. I tried thinking of acts we could do.

'What about doing a play?' I suggested. 'I'm the detective and you're criminals I have to catch.'

Bernadette made a face but said, 'OK, so what crimes have we committed?'

I said I'd have to work that out, and started thinking frantically. Maybe we could have Chiquita tied up as if she was kidnapped, with Bernadette playing the evil kidnapper, and me, the brave detective, could be solving clues to find the hideout...

As I was thinking, a car playing loud music parked on the road outside. Bored with waiting for me to invent some crimes, Chiquita started doing a dance to it. Then, because the thinking wasn't going very well, I joined in. Tara went wild, jumping around barking like he was trying to dance too.

Bernadette laughed. 'That's the worst dancing I've ever seen.'

Then Bernadette started dancing to the music, as if it had been her job to be an amazing dancer since she was born. She moved every inch of her skinny arms and legs in rhythm; she acrobatically flipped backwards then forwards; she leaped into the air, landed doing the splits and flicked around some more.

Chiquita looked at me. I looked at Chiquita.

'Bernadette, you've got a talent! You could win the contest!'

She stopped dancing immediately.

'Don't be stupid.'

'But you have to,' I pleaded. 'You're a brilliant dancer.'

'No, I'm not. I was just messing around. I don't even like pop music.'

'You have to like it if you can dance like that,' Chiquita said.

'Let's put your name down on the list right now,' I said.

'I can't.' Bernadette looked at the ground, upset. 'I can't go out there on a stage on my own. I'll feel too embarrassed. And I'll also die.'

I couldn't believe she was throwing away our chance like this. Chiquita looked as though she was going to start crying – something Chiquita usually did if she was stressed or frustrated. Or happy. Or angry. Or bored. Or . . .

Sister Finton and Sister Legori ran out to see why Tara was barking. The car with the music must have moved away, because Tara was now sitting quietly, although he was panting a lot.

Sister Finton looked at us accusingly. 'What was wrong with Tara?'

'He was dancing,' I said. 'And I think he was singing.'

Both little nuns clapped their hands delightedly. 'Oh, he does that – he loves a song and dance. That's why we can't play a radio in the kitchen or we're driven mad by Tara's performing.' They patted Tara and went back in.

27

'That dog is mad,' Bernadette said, looking at Tara and shaking her head.

'But funny,' I realized. And had a great idea. 'What about if it was Bernadette and the dancing dog? Then you wouldn't be alone on stage.'

'No. Anyway, you two dancing was even funnier. Why don't you dance with the dog as a comedy act?'

'No' – suddenly I saw the answer – 'we'll all do it!' We'd get some really cool track for Bernadette to dance to, doing all her impressive flipping around, then halfway through, me and Chiquita and Tara would come out like backing dancers and be ridiculous. Bernadette would just carry on being cool, trying to pretend we weren't there, until finally she'd give in and deliberately dance as badly as us.

I think I'd stolen the idea from some ancient comedy programme my grandad used to watch, but never mind.

Bernadette said she'd feel better if it wasn't meant to be serious. 'I mean, the thing is,' she added, frowning, 'dancers are supposed to be good-looking.'

Right away, Chiquita said a brilliant thing: 'When you're dancing you look more than good. You look like a star.'

Bernadette was pleased, although she carried on frowning and looking awkward. 'Maybe I'll do it then. If I'm not on my own.'

I promised her we'd be there, clowning around, keeping her company.

'OK.' Bernadette nodded. 'As long as it looks like it's meant to be a joke. Then no one can laugh at me.'

I think I understood what she meant. Bernadette knew her image in school was as grumpy, swotty and sporty – it would be nerve-racking to go out on stage suddenly wanting people to see her as cool and fashionable. She'd feel safer with us there beside her, fooling around. Even though she didn't really need us. Once people saw her dance, they'd very quickly see she was naturally cool, and have to accept it.

But never mind all that complicated stuff: the main thing was, we would thrash Danielle in the contest for sure.

I thought Bernadette was looking for new excuses to get out of it when she started worrying that the kitchen nuns wouldn't let Tara join in, but they said it was fine.

'Although you have to be very careful he's on his lead when he's anywhere near an open door or a gate, or he'll be off like a rocket . . .'

So we decided we'd get two long leads, me and Chiquita holding one each while we were dancing with Tara. That way it would look even funnier and Tara would be safe from turning into a rocket.

CHAPTER FIVE

'Dance routine?' Danielle read out from the list. 'You lot?'

'Bernadette's a fantastic dancer,' Chiquita said.

'Oh, we'll see about that,' Danielle sneered.

On the list beside her name, where she'd written: *Piano playing and song*, she added: *and dance*. Then she smirked at us and said, 'I'm probably the best dancer, don't you think?'

There wasn't much I could say except, 'No, I don't think so.'

And Bernadette looked as though steam might come out of her ears.

Danielle just laughed and, to make her point, ran down the corridor and turned a cartwheel before she ran out of the door.

'Cartwheels?' Bernadette looked horrified. 'I can't do that.'

'If you can do back flips, you can do cartwheels,' Chiquita said firmly.

But when Bernadette tried practising cartwheels, she just collapsed in a heap. For some reason she could only be acrobatic backwards and forwards, not sideways.

'Never mind,' Chiquita said. She seemed to have taken charge of directing our show. 'If you flip backwards and forwards really fast it'll look much better than stupid cartwheels. Anyway, cartwheels isn't dancing, it's a sport thing.'

But I had a nasty feeling that cartwheels would impress Sister Vincent, the chief judge and sports teacher.

The next day Toby arrived with a cameraman called Clive and the reality-TV show filming started. Even if sharks and whales had come up the plugholes and into their baths, people wouldn't have been interested; all anyone cared about was the filming. Girls who were usually scruffy fussed about with their hair and getting stains off their uniforms. Girls who were usually quiet and shy talked very loudly whenever they saw the film crew was near, desperate to attract attention. It was a bit pointless, though, as the cameraman, Clive, always seemed to be concentrating on Danielle.

They filmed Danielle explaining about the school. They filmed Danielle playing hockey. They filmed Danielle talking about the talent contest. They filmed Danielle having singing lessons. They filmed Danielle introducing some of the other girls; quite a lot of the other girls – but not us.

Then they filmed some lessons, some meal times ... I was pretty sure they were filming every girl and nun and fly in the school – but not us.

Also, Toby was very good-looking, so annoyingly Danielle could show off about that as well. Some of her crowd got all giggly around him, and I noticed the older girls started wearing make-up on filming days and complaining that it was stupid to film our class so much.

Clive the cameraman was older, squash-faced, slightly bald, and had a tattoo of a sun on his neck – none of these things made girls get giggly around him. He just grunted when Toby spoke to him and filmed what he was told to film. I started to wonder if he could talk at all. Then one day he surprised me. He was fixing one of his cameras in the corridor outside our classroom and he said, 'I was listening to you reading something out in class. You sound like a London kid.'

I said I was.

'Yeah, you don't sound as posh as the rest of them. But your parents are rich, right?'

'No. There's just my mum. But I had a mad auntie who died and left money for me to go to this school.'

'A mad auntie?' He laughed. He had a very strong London accent as well, by the way, so at first I thought that's what made him talk to me.

'She was a bit mad, definitely.'

He laughed again. 'If she could pay for this school, she must have been rich as well as mad.'

'I think she was very rich,' I said. 'She made tons of money with a cleaning company called Apricot Services. Maybe you've seen her cleaners. They have apricot-coloured uniforms and hats.'

You might wonder why I was telling Clive the camera-man all this about my auntie. The truth is, I was desperate. My auntie's cleaning company was one of the biggest in London, so I thought maybe this would make me seem interesting. Maybe they'd want to film me talking about it.

Clive the cameraman shook his head. 'Apricot-coloured uniforms and hats? Don't think I've seen that.'

He looked as though he was going to walk away, so I did something desperate. I panicked and told him the one thing I shouldn't have told him about my auntie's cleaning company.

'All kinds of people worked there, even Chiquita's mum.'

I pointed out Chiquita, who was leaning against a radiator in the corridor, eating chocolate and looking at a fashion magazine, something she did nearly all the time, if she wasn't crying or sleeping.

Clive was confused. 'She's here but her mum's a cleaner?'

'Oh, not any more; her mum's a famous model now but she used to work for my auntie when she was young.'

Clive was staring at Chiquita. 'Who's her mum then?'

'Stella Diaz.'

Clive stared at Chiquita a bit more. Then he looked amazed. 'Of course. She looks like her, like a little, less-beautiful version of her.'

'Don't say that – she gets upset if people say that.'

'Oh, sure, sure, of course I wouldn't say that,' he said, and then stared at Chiquita again. 'So Stella Diaz has a secret daughter.'

'It's not a secret,' I said. 'They didn't find each other until a month or so ago because Chiquita was sort of kidnapped.'

'Really? How much was the ransom?'

Then I had such a bad feeling. I knew I shouldn't have told Clive any of this, no matter how much I wanted to get his attention. He was too interested. I realized he could be a kidnapper. Otherwise why was he asking how much the ransom was? He'd pretended to be a cameraman and come to our school looking for a rich girl to kidnap . . .

To put him off, I should have told him the weird truth: that Chiquita had been kidnapped by a mad nun and there was no ransom money involved, but my head was all in a spin with what I'd just done.

He was asking me again: 'How much was the ransom? What happened?'

Maybe he wouldn't be put off now anyway. He knew Stella Diaz was mega-rich and now he'd found out who her daughter was . . . I wanted to tell him I was on to him and he'd better watch out. I'd tell him I'd be keeping an eye on him in case of kidnapping because Chiquita had only just been unkidnapped, so she didn't really need it happening again.

But before I could say any of these heroic things, I heard Toby calling.

'Clive, Clive! Where are you? I want to shoot this interview with the headmistress now, Clive, now!'

And Clive had to go off. I notice he made a very, very irritated face, as if he didn't like Toby at all. But perhaps he was just irritated at being interrupted now he'd found out who to kidnap.

CHAPTER SIX

Clive might be a kidnapper but he was quite useful in another way. He must have told Toby who Chiquita was because suddenly they wanted to film us. This didn't mean there'd be no kidnapping – possibly Toby, brother of the evil Danielle, was in on it too. We'd have to see.

Before filming our rehearsals, Toby wanted to do an interview with Chiquita – not me and Bernadette. She was the worst of us to interview, because she just said 'Yes'; 'No'; 'Don't know' – and then they started asking her about how come she only just found her mother, and she started crying . . .

Sister Ita clapped her hands and said, 'That's enough interviewing, just film their rehearsals now.'

There was always a nun keeping an eye on the interviews because we were only eleven and we might get upset. This was probably only true in Chiquita's case. Personally I'd have been very un-upset to be interviewed on television, but no one was interested in me.

Our rehearsals went quite well. Bernadette danced a great dance. Even though she was tearful, Chiquita pulled herself together and clowned around well with me and Tara. Toby, Clive and Sister Ita laughed and said we were very entertaining.

When they left us alone in the back yard and Tara was lying down panting, Chiquita said, 'You're smart, Katie. It was a great idea to tell them about my mum – that's so much more interesting than anything about Danielle. OK, I'd like to be famous by myself one day, but for now it's a great way to get us in the documentary more than Danielle.'

I didn't let on that telling Clive the cameraman about her mum could have been a dangerous mistake because he could be a kidnapper … But still, before anything bad happened we'd got the good thing of Danielle being completely livid when she heard that we'd been filmed.

She was. That evening in study, Sister Vincent had to go out and left us to do our homework 'without talking', but of course we did.

Me and Chiquita were asking Bernadette to explain the impossible maths homework when Danielle suddenly whispered loudly to Chiquita, 'I think it's disgusting that someone as boring as you got in the documentary just because your mum's interesting.'

Chiquita burst into tears.

Bernadette said, 'Shut up, Danielle.'

And I said, 'You're only in the documentary because Toby is your brother.'

'At least I've got a brother, and a father,' Danielle said, because she was one of those people who always said the most hurtful thing she could think of.

I was so furious I nearly jumped across the desk and started a fight but Bernadette grabbed me and whispered, 'Don't do anything – ignore her, we can't get in trouble!'

Unfortunately she was right.

Danielle laughed. 'Oh, yes, better not get in trouble or you can't be in the talent contest with your stupid act.' Then she turned to Indira and said, 'You should see it – they dance with the kitchen nuns' smelly old dog.'

Bernadette squeezed my arm, partly to keep me calm, partly to stop herself fighting Danielle.

Then, to my surprise, Indira said, 'Maybe the nuns' dog is a good dancer.'

There was a pause. Everyone was shocked, especially Danielle. Indira usually just stood around looking elegant and agreeing with Danielle.

'It's half blind and it smells,' Danielle said, disgusted.

'Nevertheless,' Indira said, because she always used a very fancy way of talking, 'it may have unexpected abilities, as indeed might Bernadette, Katherine and Chiquita.'

Which I think meant we might be good.

'Really, Indira,' Danielle said, 'I don't think you

know what you're talking about – you haven't even seen them.'

'Nor have you,' Indira said quietly.

'My brother, the programme director, told me all about it. I have to tell you he was laughing his head off when he was describing it.'

'It's meant to be funny,' I said, because I couldn't keep the ignoring thing going.

'There, you see, Danielle, they intend it to be amusing,' Indira said.

Danielle was obviously so furious that Indira was daring to argue, she totally lost it with her so-called friend and said, 'Oh, next you'll tell me your boring poem's meant to be funny.'

Indira looked as if she'd like to call her father's guards to behead Danielle. I don't know if her father had beheading guards, but Indira was a princess, so you never know.

'Danielle,' she said quietly and haughtily, 'at times you are a deeply unpleasant person and, for your information, my entry in the contest is a scene from an Indian play, not a poem.'

Danielle just made a spiteful smile. 'Indira, whatever it is, how many times have I got to tell you it's totally boring?'

Some girls who still liked Danielle started laughing. Indira looked at me as if she wanted me to help her out. I couldn't think of anything to say. Bernadette folded her arms, her little freckly face all pointy with anger.

'Well, Indira, at least now you know: Danielle is a big bouncy blonde cow.'

Indira smiled.

'Don't say that, Bernadette. For many people in India the cow is a sacred animal, to be respected. One can hardly respect Danielle.'

'Well, that's you cut out of the documentary, loser,' Danielle snapped at Indira.

'Oh, boo hoo,' said Indira, and carried on with her homework. She looked calm but her pen was digging hard into the paper, showing how upset she really was.

Danielle must have panicked that if she'd lost Indira as a friend, she might have lost all her friends, so she announced loudly, 'For those of you who are interested, Toby wants to film us going for a walk on Saturday, so anyone who wants to replace Indira as my partner on the walk can see me after study.'

I got on with my impossible-to-understand maths and hoped no one would want to walk with Danielle on Saturday.

But of course they did – loads of creeps stood around her after study wanting to walk with her.

Indira walked to the bedrooms alone, looking really miserable. The more I thought about it, the more it seemed amazing that she'd suddenly been on our side against Danielle. I ran to catch up with her.

'Thanks for standing up for us,' I said. 'It was a big surprise.'

Indira stopped walking and smiled sadly. 'I was going to have an argument with Danielle anyway. She's been telling me I should drop my "boring" act and just be her assistant for the talent contest. Maybe my act isn't very interesting, but why shouldn't I try to do something on my own?'

I nodded. 'She thinks nobody else could possibly be as talented as she is.'

'She might be right,' Indira said, 'but I can't abide bad manners, and calling my act "boring" was extremely bad manners.'

'And horrible,' I added.

She shook her head. 'No. The most horrible thing is that now, after I've finally had the big argument with Danielle that I've wanted to have for days, I still have to share a room with her.'

I thought of offering to get her more eggs to put in Danielle's bed, but maybe that wouldn't have been Indira's style.

'You can walk with me on Saturday,' I said to try and help.

'I thought you and Bernadette were inseparable,' she said with a nice smile.

'Well, yes, but then there's Chiquita too, so if you're our friend, it'll be better – we'll be an even number.'

'You mean I may join your gang?' Indira said, as if she thought it was quite a funny idea.

'We're not really a gang,' I said, a bit embarrassed by the childish sound of it. Although Bernadette did call us a gang and made us have a secret headquarters under a tunnel of branches in the woods. Luckily it was too cold at the moment to hide in the woods, so maybe Indira didn't need to find out about all that childishness. 'It just so happens there's three of us who want the total destruction of Danielle.'

'I don't know about total destruction,' Indira said thoughtfully, 'but I certainly have discovered her to be unnecessarily cruel and would prefer other companions.'

'What?' I asked. I hoped she wouldn't think I had bad manners but I didn't understand her.

'I mean I'd rather be friends with other people, not Danielle,' she said, smiling. 'Not now I've realized that she just uses people and pushes them around and has no manners at all.'

I told Indira I would definitely be one of her new friends and she said she was pleased. This was good, because Princess Indira was another possible candidate to be kidnapped by Clive the cameraman, so it was extremely useful if she was close at hand where I could keep an eye on her.

When I explained what was going on to Bernadette and Chiquita, they thought I was right: Indira had made an enemy of Danielle when she supported us, so it was up to us to make sure she wasn't all alone without friends. I didn't tell them about my kidnapping fears because I didn't want Chiquita to get frightened.

I just had to hope that Bernadette, who could be very bad-tempered and bad-mannered, wouldn't annoy Indira and make her go off on her own. Alone, she could be in great danger.

Rumours went around that Danielle had chosen Rachel Holmes to walk with her. Rachel had very rich parents in France and her older sister was quite a famous actress, so it was easy to see why Danielle liked her: another rich person who also had some famousness in her family to fight back at the famousness of Chiquita's mother.

But when Saturday morning came, something had happened that was far more important than who walked with who.

CHAPTER SEVEN

Sister Finton and Sister Legori gave us a bag of sweets each for helping in the kitchen all week, even though we'd had to do it anyway as a punishment.

I was just going to eat my sweets when I noticed the sell-by date was five years ago. Bernadette opened hers and said, 'Yuk!' about some mould on them.

Chiquita had already put one in her mouth and spat it out. 'Ugh,' she said. 'That's disgusting.' And Chiquita was the kind of person who'd have eaten mud if you'd told her there was chocolate inside.

'Those old kitchen nuns are mad,' Bernadette said grumpily. 'All the food they make is poisonous and now they've given us poisoned sweets.'

'They've given us sweets before,' Chiquita said. 'They were OK.'

'Yeah,' I said. 'Maybe they ran out of good ones.'

I didn't believe the kitchen nuns would do anything deliberately mean. I'd realized that they made horrible food because they just completely didn't know how to cook, and they probably forgot how long the sweets at the bottom of the box had been there.

Anyway, I wanted to get out in the back yard and practise a great new idea I'd had for Tara to take a bow at the end of the show. I was sure that if he could beg and jump and bark in time to music, he could bow.

'Bow-wow, you mean.' Bernadette laughed at her own joke.

'I don't know—' Chiquita started.

'Just a bit of a practice before it gets dark,' I pleaded.

'What about Indira?' Chiquita said. 'We said we'd meet up with her if we finished early.'

This was true, although I knew Chiquita was only making an excuse to get away and find some sweets she could eat.

I didn't want Indira left on her own, but I didn't want Chiquita wandering around on her own either. The more we stuck together, the less chance there was of a kidnapping. I said that as there wasn't much time, Bernadette might as well go with Chiquita and I'd catch up, once I'd practised a bit with Tara.

'Why don't you find Indira and bring her back here?' I suggested.

'I'm too tired,' Bernadette said. 'It's all right for you, just fooling around, but my dance is very tiring.'

I didn't say anything about how fooling around in an

organized and funny way was more tiring than she might think. I wanted them to hurry up and find Indira. I went back into the kitchen.

There was no one there. All the big pots and pans were scrubbed and put away, dishes stacked ready to be put out in the morning. Tea towels were washed and hanging up to dry over the big stove. Without people, the kitchen seemed too big and very lonely.

Tara stood up when he saw me pick up the CD player from the side bench. He wagged his tail, happy that there'd be some music. He wagged his tail even more when he saw me go to the cupboard where the nuns kept his biscuits. I put a couple in my pocket so I could reward him if he got the bowing right. He jumped up on me, trying to get at my pockets, but he was quite obedient when I shooed him away. For a dog that was supposed to be mostly blind, he always managed to see anything that was going to be interesting for him. Maybe he just acted blind for attention from the nuns. Mind you, I had come out one morning and found him jumping up and begging from a broom someone had left in the yard. In his blindness he'd thought it was some new, very thin person who might give him treats. Poor Tara.

I'd never had a dog but always wanted one, so I think that's why I liked trying to train Tara. Even though he was probably not the coolest dog in the universe, I'd got attached to him and his funny blind, or pretending-to-be-blind, ways.

It was getting dark. The yard with its high fence suddenly seemed a bit spooky. Bernadette was always telling stories of ghosts in the school. Or stories of live but hideously diseased killer nuns who were kept locked up but could get out and murder or strangle or— I made myself forget about that. I had to work on my new idea for our act and not be distracted by scary thoughts.

I wanted to win the contest too much. At night, before I went to sleep, I kept imagining myself being rich and famous, getting out of a limousine wearing great clothes, and there on the pavement would be a man saying, 'Excuse me, excuse me, miss, please could I just have a word? It seems strange, miss, but I think I might be your father . . .'

But without rehearsals, none of this could possibly happen.

I skipped the CD forward so it was nearly at the end of the tune we were using. Tara started jumping around and barking the minute he heard the music. When the song ended, he flopped down. The only way to make him bow, I decided, was to put a biscuit on the ground so he'd bend his head to eat it. But it just looked like a dog lying down eating a biscuit. Then I had a better idea. What if me and Chiquita said 'Thank you' at the end, but did it in funny voices like a dog howling. And maybe, because Tara howled and barked in time to things he heard, he'd bark or howl something that sounded like 'Thank you'.

So I was kneeling on the ground beside Tara, saying

'Thank you' in a dog-like howl, trying to make him copy me, when the garden gate opened and a scruffy man came in.

Tara jumped up and ran at the gate but the man shut it quickly. So it was true: Tara *could* run fast when he wanted.

The man said, 'Hello there, Tara.' Then he looked at me.

At first I was a bit embarrassed because I'd been kneeling on the ground howling like a dog. Then I was a bit nervous – I'd never seen this man before.

All my life, for as long as I remembered having ears to hear, Mum and Grandad had told me not to talk to strangers on my own. I was supposed to say 'Excuse me' and run to find an adult I knew. I was gathering myself up to do this when the man smiled.

'Are Sister Finton or Sister Legori here?' he asked politely.

Mum and Grandad always said it didn't matter how polite or kind the stranger seemed, there could be danger. And worse, no matter what he seemed like, this man could be one of Clive's kidnap accomplices. So I lied and said, 'Oh, they're around somewhere.'

Really, I should run now.

But I noticed Tara was still by the man, wagging his tail, acting as if he knew him.

'My name's George. The Sisters said they had some gardening work for me this week.'

He had a nice gentle voice but he was so scruffy I'd

almost say he was a tramp. And maybe he had biscuits in his pockets to trick Tara into liking him.

'I'll go and get them,' I said, running inside and slamming the door behind me.

The kitchen was still deserted. I didn't know where Sister Finton and Sister Legori went when they weren't in the kitchen. They weren't in the dining room either. I noticed from the dining-room clock that it was time for study. I was surprised I hadn't heard the bell go – but then I had been playing loud music and howling.

I ran out into the corridor, wondering if I should knock on the door of the nuns' section to see if anyone could help me with the possible kidnapper, who could be following me, or strangling Tara or anything bad.

I knocked. I waited, then I jumped as I heard Sister Vincent's voice at the other end of the corridor.

'You, girl, Katherine Milne, what are you doing there? You should be in evening study.'

I didn't think it was fair that she was talking in this telling-me-off tone when I'd possibly just escaped from a terrible kidnapping, strangling and so on.

'I didn't hear the bell, Sister.'

'There was a bell, whether you heard it or not, so go to study.'

'But, Sister, there's a man outside.'

'*A man?*' she said, like I'd said a talking cheese was outside.

'He says he's called George.'

'Oh, George,' she said. She obviously knew George well. 'I'll tell Sister Legori.'

She fished around in her pockets and pulled out a mobile phone. Sister Vincent had all kinds of useful things in her pockets; so many that she rattled while she walked. And I mean all kinds of things – cutlery, a whistle, a torch, string, pens, scissors, forty different keys . . . She sent a text while she was talking to me.

'George helps around the gardens sometimes. I'll let Sister Legori know he's here . . . Can you get the talent-contest lists down from the wall behind you? I need to go through them and organize the class heats.'

I took the lists off the notice board. There were loads of names.

'Good girl, good girl. Oh, but actually you're not, are you?'

'Aren't I?'

'Indeed I'd say not. You're one of the very naughty egg girls and here you are in corridors when you shouldn't be. Well, Sister Patricia's taking study tonight so I can sort out the talent contest, and I expect she's wondering where you are. Hurry along and try to behave.' She looked at her mobile phone. 'Ah, there, Sister Finton's coming to see George.'

'So he's all right, Sister? George?'

'Yes, dear. He's just George, a nice helpful chap.'

It was a bit disappointing that he was just George, and not part of some criminal plot being plotted by Clive the cameraman with the sun tattooed on his neck – I mean, that had to be a sign of something criminal, don't you think?

I ran to study. George might be a 'nice helpful chap' but there was still Clive to worry about. I could be wasting time on George when Clive had already knocked out Bernadette, kidnapped Indira and/or Chiquita and . . .

Actually, they were all sitting safely in study. Sister Patricia, who squeaked when she talked, squeaked at me and told me off for being late. Not very interesting. Very annoying, in fact, because Danielle got to smile about me being in trouble *again*.

CHAPTER EIGHT

The next morning was Saturday and we had some free time to practise with Tara. Indira had a piano lesson so I knew she was safe. As we went into the kitchen, Chiquita and Bernadette were laughing because I'd been showing them my howling-like-a-dog idea. We stopped, surprised. Sister Vincent was there, arms folded, shaking her head sadly. She was watching Sister Finton, who was sitting at the table, drinking tea, shaking her head. Sister Legori was sitting at the other side of the table, drinking tea, shaking her head and saying sadly, 'Oh dear, oh dear.'

When she saw us, Sister Vincent bellowed at us, 'What do you children want?'

A bit startled, I mumbled, 'We came to rehearse with Tara, he's in our act.'

Sister Legori looked up at us and said angrily, 'I told you about that gate.'

And Sister Finton dropped her head onto her arms and

started crying. It was a terrible sight to see a little old nun sobbing as if her heart would break.

'Now, now, Sister Finton,' Sister Vincent said vaguely.

Sister Legori hurriedly went to sit beside her and put her arm round her shoulders.

'Oh dear, Finton, oh dear,' she said over and over.

Sister Vincent stepped over to us, glaring. 'You are the children who play with the dog?'

'Rehearse with it,' I said.

'Never mind that. The point is, you were told the animal would bolt if the gate was left open. Sister Finton and Sister Legori trusted you with their animal and now their animal has bolted.'

It took me a few seconds to understand that when she said 'bolted', Sister Vincent meant that Tara had run off. This was terrible. It was terrible that Tara had run off. It was terrible that the kitchen nuns were so upset. But what was *most* terrible was that they thought it was our fault.

'Sister,' I explained, 'the last time I saw Tara was last night, when she was in the yard with George, gate closed.'

'Who's George?' Bernadette asked. I hadn't told her, because he hadn't seemed interesting once he wasn't a kidnapper.

Sister Finton looked up. Her little eyes were all puffy from crying. 'I spoke to George about doing some gardening. He shut the gate after he left. Tara was here. He went into his kennel to sleep. That's the last time I saw him.'

'Well, we haven't been in the yard in the night,' I said. 'This is the first time we've been here since yesterday.'

'No need for an impudent tone,' Sister Vincent said.

'But it can't have been us, Sister.'

Actually, I only knew it couldn't have been me, but Chiquita and Bernadette shook their heads, so I hoped they weren't lying.

Sister Finton dabbed her eyes with a little scrumpled-up tissue. 'Of course, dear. I'm sorry, I'm just so upset.'

'Tara was there this morning,' Sister Legori said. 'I took him some scraps while we were making the breakfast. I thought the children must have been out there between then and now.'

'We weren't, honestly,' Chiquita said, and nearly started crying.

I realized this was a horrible crime done to old nuns and I had to save them. 'So Tara went missing some time between then and now, ten o'clock? That's about two hours during which the crime could have been perpetrated,' I said.

Sister Vincent gave me a funny look, but I knew I was using proper detective talk.

'Crime?' Sister Legori asked, looking alarmed.

'Well, leaving the gate open was a crime, I think, Sister,' I said, and Sister Legori nodded.

Disappointingly they weren't going to let me carry on with my good start as detective on the case.

'Well, you children will have to go and practise in the hall or in your classroom,' Sister Vincent said. 'We'll let you know when Tara is found.'

'But, Sister, surely we can help?' I pleaded.

I could see Sister Vincent was going to say 'no' but she was interrupted. A policeman came into the kitchen with Sister Ita.

'Sister Vincent, the officer has some bad news,' Sister Ita said. Her normally tomato-red face was as pale as mine.

The policeman looked awkward, as if he was confused to be in a kitchen full of old nuns and schoolgirls.

'I'm afraid we've found your dog,' he said quietly.

It seemed as though everyone in the room held their breath. The policeman looked at the ground, looked up and then continued: 'Your dog was all the way down on the main road. We've got him in a blanket in the van outside.'

'In a blanket?' Sister Legori asked, her voice trembling.

'I'm afraid he ran onto the road and was hit by a lorry. If it's any consolation, he died instantly.'

Sister Finton started sobbing out awful little choking sounds. Sister Legori stared at the policeman.

'Poor Tara,' said Sister Ita.

The policeman shifted around – he looked almost as upset as we were. I felt as though all the world had turned grey. How could Tara just be dead?

I wanted the policeman to be a bad dream. But he was

there for real, looking at the ground, waiting for someone to say something.

Finally Sister Vincent spoke. 'Thank you, Officer,' she said. Then she smiled sadly at us. 'Now, you children had better go about your business.' They all stood still and silent, waiting for us to leave the kitchen.

I glanced back at Sister Finton and Sister Legori, both with their hands over their faces, crying.

Out in the corridor, Bernadette muttered, all bewildered, 'Tara's dead.' And, unusually, she looked as though she might start crying.

Chiquita was staring into space. She said sadly, 'I remember Sister Ita told me once that Tara was like a child to Sister Finton and Sister Legori. They got him when he was a puppy and treated him like he was their child.'

Chiquita had been at the school a very long time and knew all kinds of sad little secrets about the nuns.

'Who's George? Who left the gate open?' Bernadette asked, angry now, not tearful.

I explained about George, leaving out the kidnapper imaginings, and said, 'Those poor old nuns. We'll find out who killed Tara and make them pay the price.'

'What price?' Chiquita asked, because she was always a bit obsessed with money.

'Whatever the punishment is for dog-killing,' I said, and started thinking about detection methods. I could only hope the policeman was going to take fingerprints off the gate – that would be a first vital clue. Secondly . . . Then suddenly I couldn't think straight any more. Tears washed up from inside me and I ran to lock myself in the bathroom. I hated anyone to see me crying that much, even my best friends. I wanted to stay in the bathroom all day; not talk to anyone, not do any stupid school things like go on the Saturday afternoon walk.

I thought a lot about my grandad, what he'd have said to me about Tara. I imagined him sitting by the electric fire in his council flat, wearing his scruffy old slippers, telling me something wise and kind. Then I remembered: he wouldn't be by his fire any more, his life had changed completely.

As I mentioned, when she was poor, Chiquita's mum, Stella Diaz, had been a cleaner for my mad Auntie Apricot, Grandad's sister. Auntie Apricot had been very kind to Stella, so Stella liked our family and recently she had sort of adopted Grandad. He was called her Chief of Security. He went everywhere with her, keeping all her younger bodyguards in order and checking there were no murderers or journalists hiding in her hotel rooms.

I was glad he had this adventurous job now, but I missed him. When I thought of him, I thought he would be in his armchair by his fire, watching a crime programme on television. Or I'd picture him in his uniform, doing his dull old job as a security guard at Boots, guarding the tooth-paste. But he would actually be in New York, or California, or somewhere fancy, checking arrangements were safe for

Chiquita's mum. Not the same grandad I had in my mind at all.

After about half an hour Bernadette knocked on the bathroom door. I opened it. She was there with Chiquita and Indira. Chiquita was holding out her mobile phone – something we weren't supposed to have, by the way.

'I got your grandad,' Chiquita said, and handed me the phone.

They went away and I talked and talked to Grandad about Tara.

'You will be sad for a long time,' he said. 'But whenever the sad thoughts come into your head, you have to keep busy, find something else to do so thoughts of that will fill up your head instead.'

Then he told me he missed me and he'd see me soon. By the time the call ended I did feel better because I was thinking about Grandad, not Tara. I found my friends and we started to make a chart of detecting things we could do to solve the crime. Keeping busy.

Indira said we should ask every girl in the school where they'd been at the time Tara disappeared.

'"Canvassing", that's called,' I said, because I'd seen it in Grandad's TV detective programmes loads of times. 'Very good suggestion. We write down what they say and then put a star beside anyone suspicious.'

We ran to our desks to get notebooks and pens, then started with the top class, being brave, deciding anyone who told us to 'get lost' was suspicious and deserved a star. Before we knew it, we were halfway through the school, had nineteen possible suspects, and it was time for lunch. Grandad had been right – being busy was the answer.

CHAPTER NINE

By the afternoon it was pouring with rain and we couldn't go for our usual long Saturday walk in the hills. This was great because the walk was tiring, boring and freezing cold at this time of year. Bernadette, Chiquita and Indira went into the hall to get on with canvassing and I quickly headed for the kitchen to try and find out what the police were doing. In the corridor I heard Toby arguing with Sister Vincent. I ducked behind a large statue so I could eavesdrop. Toby was very annoyed as he had brought two extra helpers to film a big outdoor thing like the walk.

'Can't they just walk a bit?' he said. 'I've got an extra cameraman up here to get the scenery.'

Sister Vincent said, 'No, I'm sorry. I am responsible for these children and if they all caught colds, it would be my fault.'

Toby stomped off saying he was very disappointed and he'd get Danielle to organize a game of indoor rounders in the hall so there was something to film.

'Lovely,' said Sister Vincent, and went into her office, shutting the door with a bang.

I hurried into the kitchen, where Sister Finton and Sister Legori were drinking tea and making a big wreath out of plastic flowers.

They looked at me as if they didn't want me to be there.

'I am sorry about Tara,' I said.

Sister Finton just nodded and carried on with the plastic flowers.

'Really,' I said awkwardly. 'Me and my friends think it's just terrible.'

'Oh, I know, my darling,' said Sister Legori. 'A terrible thing.' She stood up from the table and tried to look cheerful. 'Now let me see if I can find a cup of lemonade and a biscuit for you, to make up for being so cross with you.'

'It really wasn't us that did it.' I said 'us' again, just hopeful about Chiquita and Bernadette. No, it couldn't be them. And I hadn't left them behind with Indira because I thought they were guilty: sometimes on a crime-solving mission it was easier to be on my own. For instance, if all three of us had tried to duck behind the statue, we'd have been caught. Anyway, they did all seem to think I knew best at detecting matters so it seemed logical that I would be the one who'd be finding out what the police were doing. I'd also told them that it would probably be better to stick together for the canvassing, in case people got rude. Hopefully that way they'd be safe from kidnapping for ten minutes or so. Eventually I'd have to tell them about the kidnapping danger but Chiquita was so prone to panic ... Maybe I'd just tell Bernadette first.

Meanwhile, back in the kitchen, Sister Legori was smiling a kind, beardy smile at me. 'I know, dear. I know it wasn't you,' she was saying as she got me lemonade and biscuits.

'George is going to make a little coffin and a grave for Tara,' Sister Finton said. 'And later we'll order a stone. We thought if we made a wreath out of plastic flowers then there'd always be some sort of flowers through the winter.' She looked as though she was going to cry again.

Sister Legori poured her some more tea and said, 'Finton was brought up on a farm with dogs. She's lost without Tara.'

It was all very sad but I had detecting to do.

'What have the police been doing, Sister? Did they fingerprint the gate?'

Sister Finton looked at me, very alarmed. 'Fingerprint the gate?'

'To find out who left it open.'

'They didn't do anything like that,' Sister Legori said. 'They said the lorry driver was very upset and would write us a letter but Tara had run right out under the wheels ...'

I couldn't believe the police had been so negligent in their procedures.

'But the real criminal was the one who left the gate open,' I said.

'That's true,' agreed Sister Legori. 'But they think it might have been someone attempting to break in. Some burglar came through the gate, Tara barked and he ran away, leaving the gate open.'

I hadn't thought of that. But what would he be stealing in the kitchen? Biscuits? Or maybe he came in that way to burgle the whole school. Silver sports cups and so on.

It wasn't very good if it was just some stray person trying to burgle the school – that could be anyone.

'I think that would have happened at night,' I said, 'not in the morning.'

'That's a good point,' Sister Legori said. 'Would you like another biscuit?'

'So who else would have been around the kitchen this morning?' I asked, beginning to enjoy the detective work now.

'There'd only have been George,' Sister Finton said. 'We had no kitchen helpers this morning.'

'And how trustworthy is George?' I asked.

Sister Finton looked a bit confused. Sister Legori shook her head.

'Oh, now George has been helping us for years and he's never left the gate open before.'

'Maybe something made him forget to shut it today,' I suggested.

And yet again I was embarrassed because I heard a cough behind me and realized George had come into the kitchen. I thought he might be angry that I'd accused him but he just said quietly, 'Sisters, Tara is in his coffin now, by the kennel, if you wanted to say goodbye. The lid's open if you want to put any of his things inside. Don't worry, he's wrapped in a blanket.'

'Oh, thank you, George,' said Sister Legori. 'There's hot tea in the pot – help yourself.'

Sister Legori and Sister Finton took a lead and some dog toys out of the basket under the kitchen table and scuttled out.

George sat down opposite me. With a sigh he poured some tea for himself.

I liked the way he'd spoken to the old nuns, quietly and gently. I suddenly couldn't imagine him hurting anyone or anything.

'It wasn't me who left the gate open,' he said. 'It was one of the girls.'

I had a sense of dread. What if it was one my friends?

'Which girl?' I asked him, feeling nervous about his reply.

He shrugged. 'I don't know people's names. I just help in the gardens sometimes. It's one who's been here a few years.'

I panicked. Did he mean Chiquita?

'She's got a long blonde plait, about your age.'

I quickly switched to relief. Danielle. It had to be. Oh, now the crime was really getting interesting . . .

CHAPTER TEN

I worried for a minute that I might have so badly wanted the criminal to be Danielle that I had jumped to conclusions. I asked George to describe again the girl he'd seen leaving the gate open.

Long blonde plait, about my age . . . It couldn't be anyone else.

But why had Danielle been near the kitchen? She was hardly ever in trouble and doing punishments.

'What was she doing in the back yard?' I asked George.

'Well, the thing is' – George put four sugars in his tea, taking a very long time about it – 'it looked to me like she did it on purpose.'

'Really?'

'It was odd, you know. She just ran round the side of the building, opened the gate and ran away again. I was down the end of the grounds pruning some trees so I didn't get up here in time to stop Tara.' He shrugged. 'Maybe she didn't know about Tara.'

'But she's been at the school a long time, like you said. She must have known. She must have done it on purpose.'

George nodded sadly. He was the sort of person, I could tell, who probably couldn't even imagine there'd be people as mean as Danielle in the world.

'Anyway, I tried to catch him but he was off across the fields . . . Amazing the way that old dog could run if he wanted.'

'But it's terrible,' I said. 'Why didn't you tell the nuns about Danielle?'

George shook his head. 'Those poor ladies are sad enough. Imagine how upset they'd be if they found out one of you kids did it on purpose?'

This was a good point.

George had a big dark beard and lots of dark hair, so at first it was hard to see that he had kind, clever eyes and was not a kidnapper or anything bad. And you had to wonder, considering he was probably only a bit older than my mum, why he had this weird life, looking all scruffy and digging graves for nuns' dogs in the rain as a job.

Anyway, George stood up and said he'd better get Tara buried or the poor little nuns would be standing looking at the coffin in the rain too long and get pneumonia.

I apologized for accusing him but he just smiled and shook his head.

'That's OK,' he said. 'You don't know me, you were right to be suspicious.'

'But I know now I was wrong,' I said.

He smiled again. 'I'm glad,' he said, and walked out into the rain.

I raced into the hall and found there was no detective work being done by my friends. Chiquita was sitting at the side reading magazines. Bernadette and Indira were playing rounders and being filmed along with most other people in our class.

Chiquita's chin nearly hit the floor in shock when I told her what George had said. We were bursting for the rounders to be over to tell the others. I started trying to signal.

Indira just looked puzzled, then realized the camera was on her and got distracted tilting her head in a princessy way. We couldn't even get Bernadette's attention because she was so serious about sport things. She was always wanting to show she was better than Danielle. Mainly she *was* better but she was less popular, so she always ended up with geeky, useless people on her team and lost. I mean, her best friends were me and Chiquita. And now Indira. Indira was good at hitting the ball but she didn't like to run about or do anything that might make her untidy. Chiquita hated to even move and I had a problem with the way my arms and legs always tangled up and dropped bats or balls and made me fall over. That and generally being very, very bored with any kind of sport matters.

Bernadette's team did lose the match. We didn't care

about that – we were just glad it was over. Finally we could whisper the whole Danielle-lets-out-dog story.

Indira said, 'That is awful.'

Bernadette looked like she'd explode with rage. 'We have to find some way to punish Danielle and disgrace her.'

This was true, of course, but I reminded her that we had to do it in some way that wouldn't upset poor Sister Finton and Sister Legori.

We sat around, all going, 'Um,' but none of us could think of a plan. However, in the meantime, we could still get Danielle in the corridor on the way to tea.

'I need to talk to you,' I said, pulling Danielle away from her new best friend, Rachel.

'Get off my arm, stupid,' she hissed at me.

'We know what you did,' Bernadette hissed back at her.

'What, just beat your team at rounders, on camera?' Danielle smirked.

'You let Tara out,' Bernadette said.

'I don't know what you're talking about.' Danielle was as cool as cool with her lies.

'George saw you,' I said accusingly.

'Who on earth is George?' she replied grandly.

'You know George,' Chiquita said. 'He does the garden.'

'That tramp?' Danielle laughed. 'I heard he used to be a bank robber and was in prison and the only people who'll give him a job are the nuns, so who'd believe him except idiots like you?'

She laughed again and skipped off towards the dining room, her blonde plait swinging behind her.

'Is that true?' I asked Bernadette.

'I heard he used to be a brain surgeon and then went mad and ran away,' she said.

Chiquita made a tutting noise. 'The truth is, he just does odd jobs around the area and lives in a tiny house on the edge of the farm up there.'

Whatever the truth was, I didn't like the way Danielle seemed so confident she could lie her way out of her crime.

But she did worse than that.

CHAPTER ELEVEN

Halfway through tea, Sister Vincent came into the dining room with Toby. She clapped her hands and announced, 'Everybody! We have lovely news. First, I need Danielle Kirkham-Byles up here beside me. Now I know, Danielle, you wanted it kept secret, but I feel the whole school should be told.'

Danielle stood up, shaking her head and acting as if she didn't want to go and stand by Sister Vincent. She even held her hand to her face, making out she was shy.

Sister Vincent continued: 'Now some of you may already know the tragic news that the kitchen dog, Tara, much beloved of Sister Finton and Sister Legori, escaped and was killed in a road accident. But Danielle was so concerned by this sad news that she asked her brother, Toby, to help. Toby sent one of his staff into town this afternoon and the kitchen Sisters now have a lovely new Labrador puppy.'

At that moment Sister Finton and Sister Legori came

out of the kitchen with a basket, smiling and showing the puppy.

'Apparently the puppy is to be called Taratoo. You see T-O-O but it could also mean T-W-O. Which is hilarious, you'll all agree.' Sister Vincent laughed, an insane trumpeting noise like an elephant trapped in a sandwich maker, and the kitchen nuns squeaked with giggles. Then Sister Vincent noticed that no girls were laughing at all and stopped making her elephant noise. She looked slightly pink and confused, then she said quickly, 'So it only remains to say thank you very much, Danielle and Toby.' Sister Vincent started clapping, then everyone in the dining room started clapping except me, Chiquita, Indira and Bernadette.

'I think I'm going to throw up,' said Bernadette.

I didn't think I'd throw up but I thought my head might fly off, I was so angry about Danielle's total sneaky evilness. Such total evilness that I couldn't think what I'd do about it.

I told Bernadette we had to have an emergency meeting after study. We were losing the war with Danielle like totally pathetic losers.

Not only that. Before the horrifying new-dog revelation, me and Chiquita had been sneaking around to watch people rehearsing their various acts. Most people were just practising in their bedrooms or in empty classrooms. Danielle was using the music room because she was singing and playing the piano, with a bit in the middle when she jumped up and did acrobatic dancing. Unfortunately, it was brilliant.

Another girl called Emma had quite a nice voice and was doing a song that had been in the charts a few months ago, but she wasn't as good as Danielle. Sarah and Fiona, two girls who were nice but as dull as stones, had got a comedy-sketch book from a TV show. They were doing some sketches very badly and I'm afraid to say they were the unfunniest thing you ever saw. Another girl, Clare, was playing the flute – probably playing it well, but who cared?

The more I looked at our act, the more I realized that our silly bad dancing was only really funny to us, especially now we didn't have Tara, and Bernadette was the best bit. But she kept refusing to do it without us.

The rainy afternoon turned into a stormy evening, with crashes of thunder and lightning flashing across the sky.

Up in our room, me and Bernadette drew the curtains because the lightning was making us nervous. Then we had our emergency meeting about what to do about Danielle. We'd invited Indira to the meeting, now that she was one of us.

'Really this sort of important meeting should be in our headquarters,' Bernadette said when Indira settled into a chair.

I felt embarrassed. 'Never mind about all that.'

'What's the headquarters?' Indira asked.

'It's a den in the woods,' Chiquita said. 'A dirty pile of branches that only Bernadette cares about.'

'Shut up,' Bernadette said.

'Well, perhaps I might suggest we find a better head-quarters for the inclement weather,' Indira said.

'The what weather?' Chiquita asked.

'She means in winter,' Bernadette said – luckily, because I didn't know what Indira meant either, and didn't like to say.

'Where would be the best place for a winter den? I wonder.' Bernadette frowned.

I could see she was going to get completely distracted with dens and not think about the important matters.

'We have to think about defeating Danielle above all other things to think,' I said.

Bernadette didn't carry on with her den rubbish and said, surprisingly calmly, 'I expect you're right.'

Indira nodded. 'It's dreadful that just because she's so rich she can get out of trouble by buying a bribe dog.'

'That's it exactly,' said Bernadette. 'It's a bribe dog.'

'How much does a dog cost?' Chiquita asked, off in some dog-shopping dream.

'Well, I expect they can afford it,' Indira said. 'Her family do own practically half of Scotland.'

'Well, I'm glad I'm not in their family. Their house is weird,' Chiquita said, coming back down to earth. 'It's not a house really. More like a castle. With all stuffed deer's heads on the walls and suits of armour.'

'And,' Bernadette said, 'those suits of armour aren't hollow inside. They've bought super-expensive robot soldiers to put inside. So if anyone attacks the family, they hunt them down, never tiring, on and on, slashing through doors with their swords—'

'What are you talking about?' Indira looked at Bernadette as if she was mad.

But I knew Bernadette was getting started on one of her great scary stories, so I encouraged her.

Outside the thunder rumbled and the rain slashed at the windows, almost as hard as the swords of robot soldiers.

'What else is in their castle, Bernadette?' I asked.

'It's all big wooden staircases lit by flaming torches. As you go up and up, past the paintings of dead ancestors and the deer's heads on the walls, you finally reach the top floor. The execution floor.'

There was a huge crash of thunder outside and we all jumped.

'Execution floor?' Chiquita frowned. 'I don't remember that.'

Many years ago she'd been friends with Danielle and spent a half-term at her house, so she did know what was in it for real.

'They don't show it to visitors,' Bernadette said. 'Visitors are always treated nicely. But what they don't know is that up on the top floor there is a chopping block and a huge axe. This is where Mr Kirkham-Byles chops off the heads of any of his enemies or servants who disobey him. He chops off their heads, buries the bodies in the garden, then stuffs the heads. Oh yes – up on the execution floor the walls are lined not with stuffed deer's heads but with human heads, staring, horrified, their mouths open in an eternal scream—'

At that moment we all screamed because the lights went out.

There was no need for panic.

In a few seconds the lights came on again.

'I expect the storm is affecting the power supply,' Indira said sensibly.

'Or it's the robot soldiers cutting the cables,' Bernadette said in a horror-film voice.

'Stop it, Bernadette,' Indira said, hugging on to a pillow. 'You're making me most uneasy.'

'Anyway,' said Chiquita, 'if they had whole loads of people with chopped-off heads, they'd be in jail by now.'

'No, no.' Bernadette shook her head. 'They're so rich they can do what they like. Just like buying the nuns a new dog, the Kirkham-Byles buy policemen new sports cars and judges new houses ... They'll go on and on with their murderous ways – no one can ever defeat them.'

'Just like we can't defeat Danielle,' I added.

'Well, I think we should put far-fetched stories to one side,' said Indira, 'and work out a proper plan.'

I was a bit annoyed with her then because I was sure Bernadette had more gory, disgusting things to tell us about if Indira hadn't kept interrupting with sensibleness.

'Yes. Fine,' said Bernadette, who was obviously also annoyed. Then, as the thunder rattled the bedroom windows, she added, 'Although it's worth remembering that the Kirkham-Byleses' castle is surrounded by buried headless corpses rotting away and in a few generations they'll all be poisoned by the stinking fumes, so eventually their own evil will defeat them.'

'Bernadette, even if that were true' – Indira sighed – ' "in a few generations" and "eventually" doesn't help us with Danielle.'

'No,' Bernadette admitted. 'In the meantime Danielle the monster, from a long line of monsters, might as well be chopping off our heads and stuffing them, she's defeating us so much.'

Chiquita was off in a bit of a dream again. 'What do they stuff the heads with?' she asked.

'Cotton wool,' Bernadette snapped. 'Like inside your head.'

'Inside my head?' Chiquita laughed. 'You're the one with a lot of mad stories stuffing your head. You should be rehearsing your dancing to beat Danielle, not thinking up robot stories.'

Bernadette made a face. 'We won't beat her in the talent contest – you know we won't – so what's the point?'

'That's not the attitude,' Indira said. 'I think we should all stop talking nonsense and rehearse our acts. That's the only positive thing we can do.'

It was boring but she was right. While Indira went off somewhere to rehearse, we got in line and practised our moves.

We kept being put off by the way the lights were flickering. We had no music so Chiquita sang the song very badly, which was also off-putting.

And I didn't like Indira being alone, wandering in a storm where possible kidnappers might lurk. I should have at least checked where she was going.

Eventually, despite all this, we were working hard and so busy falling over our own feet that we didn't notice Danielle standing in the doorway.

'How long have you been there?' Bernadette growled when she saw her.

Danielle just stood there, smirking with her arms folded. 'Long enough to see you practising your dreadful act,' she sneered.

'Get lost, dog-killer,' Bernadette shouted, and threw a pillow at her. It surprised her but probably didn't hurt her enough, so I threw a pillow too.

'Yeah, killer, liar!' I yelled.

Danielle ducked. The pillow flew past her and hit Sister Vincent, who was coming in the door.

'What? A pillow!' Sister Vincent said, catching it and staring at it as if she'd never seen one before. Then she looked at us as if she'd never seen us before. 'Why are you children throwing pillows? What is the matter with you?'

We didn't say anything. Sister Vincent put the pillow on the bed and then put her hands on her hips.

'Well, speak, somebody. Who threw the pillow? Come on, quickly now, who did it?'

'I'm sure they know they have to own up, Sister,' Danielle said meekly, putting on an angelic face.

'I did it,' said Bernadette, who always owned up. So I had to own up as well.

Sister Vincent looked at us for a moment, shaking her head. 'Didn't I tell you what would happen? That's it, no talent contest for you two.'

'For throwing pillows?' Bernadette protested.

'That's not fair on Chiquita,' I said desperately. 'She didn't throw anything and we're all in the act together.'

Sister Vincent looked at me, then asked Chiquita: 'Is this true, Chiquita?'

'I can't do an act on my own,' she said, starting to cry. 'I'm just there to help Bernadette, I can't do anything on my own.'

'Oh, Chiquita, Chiquita, don't cry. Oh heavens, whoever saw such a child for crying. Very well, very well. We'll send them to help in the kitchen for another week, then see how their behaviour looks. Now come along, Danielle, I have your mother on the telephone. Apparently there's a problem with the costume you ordered.'

Danielle smirked as she went away, delighted with the new damage she'd done.

We counted ourselves lucky to still be in the contest but were a bit disturbed to hear that Danielle had a costume.

'I didn't even think of costumes,' Bernadette groaned.

'I know where we can get some.' Chiquita ran off towards her room.

We followed her and found her talking on her secret mobile phone. She was speaking to her mum. Stella Diaz was bound to have lots of brilliant ideas about costumes.

Chiquita came off the phone smiling. 'Great. I told my mum we were doing a sort of comedy acrobat dancing thing. She says she'll send us ninja suits.'

Bernadette looked alarmed. 'What's a ninja suit?'

'Oh, you know,' Chiquita said. 'Really cool loose black trousers and jackets, with headbands. She said she'd get silk ones – quite expensive but really elegant. It's always worth paying for quality, don't you think?'

Bernadette just stared at her.

I didn't care about Chiquita's shopping theories, but I thought it sounded like a good idea. I persuaded Bernadette that it wouldn't look silly. Well, it probably wouldn't . . .

We wondered about Danielle's costume and hoped it

wouldn't be anything interesting or cool like a ninja suit. We decided to find Indira to see if she would spy on Danielle's costume for us, seeing as they still shared a room, but Sister Ita appeared at the end of the corridor and chased us to our rooms.

'That's enough running around now. It's bed time and I hear two of you are working in the kitchen early, yet again.'

I hoped Indira was OK, but with Sister Ita standing staring at me, I couldn't do anything except go to bed.

I felt very tired from all the worrying and getting angry I'd been doing all day. I was sure I'd be fast asleep seconds after Sister Ita turned out the lights. But I lay awake for ages, listening to the thunder, imagining giant robots in armour crashing about in the gardens.

I wondered if I should ask Grandad for ideas about defeating Danielle. I didn't understand her. She was good at everything and seemed to have everything but she was so awful. If I had long blonde hair and lived in a castle with a rich mum and dad, I was sure I'd be a nice person. Then again, Chiquita, Indira and Bernadette didn't have everything and they were still nice. Well, Bernadette was nice underneath.

I tossed and turned and realized the whole world was confusing, not just Danielle. And Mum was far away, Grandad even further, so I'd just have to grow up and fight my own battles.

The wind started howling like the howls of the

Kirkham-Byleses' servants on their way to the execution floor. The more I imagined it, the more I knew I'd have nightmares.

And I did. Unlike Bernadette, who was one of those people who could think up terrifying stories then go to sleep, smiling and snoring, probably dreaming about fluffy teddy bears or something.

CHAPTER TWELVE

Back in the kitchen for our punishment, we were surprised not to see the puppy: apparently George had taken it up to the farm until it had learned not to wee on the floor.

'But we still get him for walks,' said Sister Finton, her little hairy face lit up all happily. 'He'll go for walks on a lead and that's that. No other activities.'

I must have looked disappointed.

'No dancing, I'm afraid,' Sister Finton said gently. 'And besides, it's too early to say if this is another musical dog.'

'Here he is now,' Sister Legori squeaked.

George was standing at the kitchen door with the puppy on a lead.

'Here you are, Sisters.'

The kitchen nuns rushed out and started fussing over the puppy. It was very cute. Much prettier than poor old blind Tara.

'George, do have a cup of tea,' Sister Legori said. 'And if one of you children could finish the tables and the other one put away the cooking pots, we're off for our walk.'

The little nuns hobbled off with the puppy on a lead between them.

George smiled and sat down. He picked up the teapot but it was empty.

'Uh-oh, looks like I'm too late with the tea,' he said.

'I'll make some,' I said. George was nice and I still felt guilty about accusing him of things. Also, if he had been a bank robber, he might still be a bit dangerous when he didn't get his own way. Or, if he was a brain surgeon, that could be useful, if someone's brain suddenly went wrong or something, so all in all it was best to make him my friend.

Bernadette went out to the dining room to finish the tables. I think she was nervous of George.

'Nice they've got the new dog already,' George said to me.

'Well, it would have been nicer if Danielle hadn't killed the old one,' I pointed out.

'That's true,' he said.

'I wish there was some revenge we could take on her but she's so sneaky.'

'People like that make you realize you're better off without people,' George said, staring into the distance as if he was remembering awful things people had done to him.

I suddenly felt sorry for him. And I didn't think what he said was true, not about everybody.

'There are nice people,' I said. 'My friends are nice. My

mum's nice. So's my grandad. Loads of people are nice. Just not Danielle.'

George laughed. He had a nice warm laugh. 'You're right, I'm lucky that way too. I've got a great brother and a lovely sister. It's just people like that girl . . . What did you say her name was?'

'Danielle.'

'Danielle, right. Well, it seems to me there are still too many people like that in the world.'

'I don't know. I never met anyone as awful as her before I came to this school,' I said, and it was true. People had been real bullies at my primary school and so on, but I'd never known anyone so sneaky. From a family busy murdering servants in their castle . . . Oh no, that wasn't quite true.

George was looking at me as if he was thinking about what I'd said.

'So you're quite new here, are you? Where are you from?'

'London.'

'Me too – a long time ago,' he said, and then he gave me a funny look. 'Your name's Katie?'

'Yes, people call me Katie Milk because I'm so pale. But it's Katherine Milne officially.'

George shook his head. 'Funny, you remind me of some-one I used to know years ago.'

'When you were a brain surgeon?' I thought it was

probably better to ask about this option than bank robbing.

'A what?' George spluttered.

'Sorry, but someone told me you were a brain surgeon and then . . . Well, then you weren't any more.'

'No,' he said, looking slightly confused. 'But funnily enough I was a medical student once. But I left before I was even a doctor, let alone a brain surgeon.' Then he looked totally amazed. 'How weird you said that because now I know who you remind me of – someone who was a trainee nurse while I was a student doctor.'

I started to have a very weird feeling.

'What was her name?'

George shook his head. 'Don't remember. I left and travelled all over the world for years. There are lots of things I don't remember. I had an accident working on a ship somewhere in North Africa. Gave me slight brain-damage so I get confused.' Then he smiled sadly. 'So the opposite of being a brain surgeon, really – brain-damaged. Just my memory, you know, and it makes me a bit slow on the uptake.'

My head was racing. 'Why did you leave being a doctor?'

'Just got bored, wanted to see the world. Started working on ships and kept going till the accident. Then I came up here to help my brother on the farm he'd bought. And I help the nuns with the gardens and odd jobs.'

Yes, yes, who cared about farms? What I was thinking was: my mum was a nurse, my dad had gone off mysteriously and George had very dark hair like me and said I reminded him of a nurse. My mum, obviously. It was obvious.

'George, were you ever married?'

'No,' he said. 'Never got married.'

At that point Bernadette came in from the dining room and said, 'All done.'

Then I realized I'd probably been having one of my typical moments of over-imagining. I'd heard the word 'nurse' and run crazy in my head ... But George said he had never been married.

'Then again,' George said suddenly, 'there are a lot of things I don't remember. I didn't remember I had a brother till the hospital tracked him down and told him I'd had an accident.'

'What accident?' Bernadette wanted to know.

I waved at her to be quiet. My imagination was off again ... 'So you could have been married and forgotten?'

'It's possible,' George said. 'But my brother's told me about most of the important things that I don't remember. That would be pretty important.'

'Maybe your brother didn't know you got married,' I said.

'That's possible too,' George said. Then he stood up. 'Well, not to worry, I'll make my own cup of tea.'

I'd been standing there with the box of tea bags but done

nothing. I handed them to George and said, 'Thanks, George, see you then.'

I grabbed Bernadette, running out of the kitchen with her. I had to tell her what I was thinking.

She just made a face. 'That's stupid. You've made up this whole thing just because he said you reminded him of a nurse. And anyway, why would he, by complete coincidence, be at the exact school you go to?'

But maybe it wasn't a complete coincidence. I reminded Bernadette how my mad Auntie Apricot had said in her will that I had to come to this exact school or lose my inheritance.

'Maybe, seeing as how she was rich, she hired private detectives to find my dad and knew I'd meet him if I came here.'

'Stop,' Bernadette said, holding her hands over her ears and making a face. 'Let's get Chiquita because you're driving me insane with all this.'

Chiquita at least would understand better. Her story that she'd found out her lost mum was a supermodel had seemed far-fetched but . . .

She nodded thoughtfully when we told her about George.

Bernadette got impatient. 'What are you nodding for? What does that mean?'

Chiquita shrugged. Very often, her and Bernadette were close to getting on each other's nerves, bickering and wasting time, so I had to speak up quickly: 'The thing is, Chiquita, you know for a fact that people who seem like complete strangers can very easily turn out to be your parents.'

Chiquita nodded some more. Bernadette made a huffy, impatient sound. Then Chiquita said, 'Yeah, but would you want it to be true that your dad was a beardy guy who cleans out cows and says he's a bit brain-damaged?'

Not ideal, I admitted, but at least it would be the mystery solved.

'But if he doesn't even remember being married...' Chiquita said sadly.

'And he probably left your mum before he got hit on the head,' Bernadette said. 'So maybe before he got hit on the head he wasn't very nice.'

Also true.

'All in all,' Bernadette went on, 'if you want to decide some complete stranger is your lost dad, you should pick someone better.'

I got a bit annoyed with her then. She didn't understand how I felt about this. It was just weird not to know about my dad.

In the end Chiquita, who'd thought she had no parents at all for years of her life, was much more helpful. And for someone who could be a bit dim, she had a brilliant idea.

'Why don't you ask your mum? Sneakily take a picture of George and send it to her. See what she says.'

This plan of Chiquita's seemed perfect. My mum was always saying things like, 'Oh look, love, the only good thing about him was that he gave me you,' for an answer. She'd never told me any details. But if she saw the photo of George and realized . . . Then at least she'd have to tell me everything, even if it was nothing but bad news about him being horrible before he was hit on the head.

And maybe, if she met him now he'd been hit on the head, she might see he had a good side. And maybe . . .

CHAPTER THIRTEEN

The next morning I went to work in the kitchen with Chiquita's – so she'd informed me – very expensive camera in my pocket. But George didn't show up. Or the next day, or the day after that.

Then I just had to ask Sister Finton: 'Where's George? I thought he brought Taratoo over for you to take for walks?'

'He does, dear, but we've decided the afternoons are better. We have more time then when you children are all at lessons.'

It might be better for them but it was no good to me. I thought perhaps I could lurk around the gardens every spare minute to see if George was working somewhere, stalk him and sneakily take a picture. The trouble with this was, every spare minute and break time I was supposed to be in the kitchen, not stalking in the gardens.

The only solution was for Chiquita to stalk George and take the picture. She said she'd do it but I was worried she wouldn't try very hard to find him. It was cold out in the gardens and I knew she'd rather be leaning against radiators eating chocolate.

Meanwhile our costumes arrived. The black ninja suits were nice and loose to jump around in. We had black head-bands and little black shoes to match. Indira said we looked cute but I worried we looked a bit dull. We didn't have a novelty dog any more. And although Bernadette was very good, she only danced; she didn't sing or play the piano.

Danielle sang, danced, played the piano and had a great costume covered in shiny beads. She had little glittery pumps and tied up her hair with silver ribbons. She looked like a cross between an angel and a pop star.

On Saturday afternoon we had the talent contest for our class. Everyone competing had to wait in the small chang-ing room beside the hall, squashed together. Danielle had made sure she had the only table to lay her things out on. She was laughing with her new friend, Rachel. Rachel was going to be helping Danielle by playing a backing CD and working a spotlight.

We had a CD but, of course, we hadn't thought of a spotlight.

Danielle also had a big professional case of make-up. Rachel was holding brushes for her while she put some on. They kept whispering and laughing, laughing, laughing. I don't know what was so funny except I did hear Rachel say,

'Well, we know none of these have a spectacular act, we just know it.'

Danielle noticed me eavesdropping and said, 'I bet you're scared – the whole school's waiting to be entertained and you've got nothing to offer.'

I'd peeped out into the hall and it was scary to see the whole school sitting there, fidgeting. Probably they would think we had nothing to offer but of course I said to Danielle, 'We're not scared. You should be.'

She just laughed some more.

I peeped out again, wondering if I kept looking at the audience, they might seem less scary. It didn't work.

Sister Vincent was the judge. She was sitting right at the front with a big notebook on a desk. And Toby was there, with Clive filming.

I wondered where Indira was. At least if Clive was filming, he couldn't be kidnapping her. Then Chiquita told me that Indira had rushed to the toilets saying she was so nervous she felt sick.

We were going to see if we could help her but Sister Patricia came flapping up to us, waving some papers.

'You three, you three first.'

Then I felt so nervous I thought I'd be sick. But there was no time. Bernadette made a face at me to show she was scared, then her music started and she ran out on stage. Chiquita and I held hands while we listened for the moment where we had to run on.

Here it was, time to go . . .

I looked at all the school out there in front of me and I understood what people meant when they said that they wished the earth would swallow them up.

But the earth didn't help me in that way, so I started trying to imitate Bernadette and falling over, the way I was supposed to. Bernadette danced well but she forgot to smile at the audience, just concentrated on what she was doing and scowled at everyone. I think they found that a bit off-putting.

People did laugh and clap. Everything happened as we'd rehearsed it. Nothing went wrong. It was just not a spectacular act.

Danielle's was a really spectacular act. She was so good it was like a professional was visiting the school to show us how it should be done. When she finished, everyone went wild, clapping and cheering.

But then there was an act I hadn't seen yet: Indira. She came out in a bright sari looking very beautiful. Considering she said she was sick with nerves, she was really calm and confident. She did this story from a play about a girl whose whole family had been killed in a war; she was being taken away by her enemies to be a slave and she wanted to die, but then at the end she realized her family would want her to be brave; whatever happened to her, she'd survive and be dignified.

When she finished, there was a long silence. People were

surprised that a girl of eleven had come out and done something so elegant and serious. Eventually someone started clapping, then everyone clapped hard. Not as much as for Danielle, but I thought what Indira had done was amazing. Without jumping around or showing off, she'd had us all listening to every word of this sad story . . . I bet if there was a real judge instead of Sister Vincent, they'd have decided that what Indira did was far more difficult. But maybe I was biased. I thought she should have won, not Danielle – who won, of course. It would be her from our class in the Christmas concert for parents.

Toby interviewed Danielle about how she felt about winning. She was still talking when Toby said, 'Great, thanks,' and rushed over to us, telling Clive to film us. Toby asked Chiquita how she felt about losing.

Chiquita just shrugged sulkily and said, 'It's only a stupid school concert.'

Then Bernadette seemed to have some invisible thing clang on her head and give her brain-damage and she yelled into the microphone: 'And I'd just like everyone on television to know that Danielle shouldn't have won because she killed the nuns' dog!'

She said it really loudly so everyone nearby, including Danielle and Sister Vincent, stopped what they were talking about and stared at her.

Toby looked a bit confused and said, 'Sweetheart, you're not actually live on television, we're just taping.'

'What do you mean by that, you wicked child?' Sister Vincent said, striding over.

Bernadette blurted out the whole story of George seeing Danielle and not wanting to upset the old nuns by telling them.

Toby looked at Danielle, puzzled. 'What's she talking about, Sis?'

Danielle laughed, a bit too high-pitched. 'It's just some spiteful lie because they lost.'

Clive was still filming.

'And besides,' Danielle said, 'everyone knows George isn't right in the head.'

'We don't say such things, Danielle.' Sister Vincent frowned. Then she looked very upset and said, 'I will speak to George in the morning because frankly, Danielle, I have known George for years and never known him to be a liar. If by some terrible accident you let out the dog, you should be brave and confess to it now.'

Danielle looked very shocked that Sister Vincent didn't immediately believe her.

Toby realized that Clive was still filming and said, 'Stop that, Clive!'

Clive stopped but muttered, irritated, 'I thought it was the most interesting thing that's happened all night.'

I was inclined to agree with him.

Bernadette looked happier than I'd seen her in ages, smirking at Danielle, who was saying to Sister Vincent, 'I can't believe you think I'd do such a thing, Sister. How could you think that?'

And Sister Vincent just said quietly, her voice very disappointed, 'I must talk to George, Danielle. I must find out the complete truth.'

For the first time in all this horrible business about Tara, Danielle looked worried. Worried and shocked. Maybe, just maybe, even though we didn't beat her in the talent contest, we might manage to beat her in real life.

CHAPTER FOURTEEN

It was a relief the stupid talent contest was over. We'd lost and there was no point worrying about it. We did go and tell Indira how brilliant we thought she was, though.

'Oh, thank you,' she said. 'I tried my best. Still, at least your accusations mean Danielle is fairly subdued and not crowing about her victory in our room.'

As usual with Indira, you had to take a minute to understand all the big words.

'Poor you, sharing a room with her,' Bernadette said.

'Yes,' Indira replied. 'It has become somewhat intolerable. But then, I despise this school and always have.'

Indira seemed so cool and perfectly behaved all the time that it was strange to hear she was unhappy at the school. She said that all her older sisters had been to our school. It was a tradition and no one had asked her if she liked it or not.

Bernadette liked to go on about how much she hated our school. So instead of trying to cheer Indira up, she said,

'Oh, yes, this school is the worst. As soon as my dad stops working in Hong Kong and comes back to England, I'm leaving. I hate it here.'

Bernadette always said her parents were coming back to live in England soon, but so far it hadn't happened.

Chiquita said, 'It's not that bad, Bernadette. I could have gone to live with my mum but I've stayed here for now because I like my friends here.'

'Well, you're just nuts,' Bernadette said.

'Whatever.' Chiquita shrugged.

I glared at them to stop them fighting. Then I tried to cheer up Indira, pointing out that Danielle was about to get smacked in the face with her crimes. George would tell Sister Vincent what he saw, Danielle would be disgraced and probably not allowed to be in the Christmas concert. And, as the only other act that wasn't pathetic, Indira would probably be in the concert.

'I wonder if she *will* be disgraced,' said Indira. 'One does observe that Danielle always manages to evade catastrophe.'

'I don't know about that,' Chiquita said, 'but somehow she always gets out of trouble.'

I didn't see how she could this time. But horror of pile-of-dead-dogs horrors, she did.

CHAPTER FIFTEEN

In the morning we were helping wash up, glad we were being punished because we'd be in the kitchen at the heart of the action. Sister Vincent would be in at any minute looking for George, all would be revealed and so on.

The first thing I noticed was that the puppy, Taratoo, was in her basket under the kitchen table.

What on earth was going on with this dog?

'Is Taratoo allowed in here now?' I asked Sister Finton.

'Oh, yes. George is a wonder with animals. He says she's got to be taken out regularly but she already knows not to do any business indoors.'

That was enough of that kind of talk, standing in the place where our meals were made. If I told my mum about dogs in kitchens, she'd go berserk.

'So, will George be here today?' I couldn't believe how complicated it was just to catch up with him and take a picture. Chiquita had been useless so far. But my problems were about to get more complicated.

Sister Finton said, 'Oh, no, he's away off now – that's it with George for the winter, so he says.'

The kitchen nuns had very strong Irish accents and sometimes I didn't understand what they said.

'Sorry, Sister . . . but what do you mean?'

Sister Finton smiled at me – luckily she wasn't offended. 'He told us this morning he's off to his sister's in Spain. He likes to be there for the winter. She has lots of little kiddies, which is nice for Christmas. All his nephews and nieces. Oh, no, we won't see George now till the spring.'

Sister Legori giggled. 'He hates the cold weather. We always say that's why he has all that hair. To keep the cold off.'

Yes, yes, hilarious, I thought. But now two plans were ruined – I couldn't get a photo of him and the destruction of Danielle wouldn't happen.

Bernadette was furious. She banged down a cooking pot and said, 'I can't believe this! She's going to get away with it!'

'Can't believe what, dear? What's the matter with you?' Sister Legori clucked around Bernadette like a fussing chicken.

But of course, no way could we tell them what had been done to their poor old dog.

I quickly made up a lie: 'We were just talking about something in a book we're reading.'

'Were you?' Sister Legori looked confused. 'I don't

remember talking about books. I thought we were talking about George.'

'It was something we were talking about earlier,' I said frantically, realizing I'd come up with a very low-quality excuse.

I was sort of saved when Sister Vincent came in from the dining room asking, 'Sisters, do you know where I might find George?'

'Well now, isn't that funny?' Sister Legori stroked her little beginning-of-a-beard. 'We were just talking about George. Well, I thought we were—'

'He's gone away to Spain,' Bernadette blurted out.

'Already?' Sister Vincent was obviously used to the idea that George went to Spain for Christmas.

'Yes,' Sister Finton said. 'He left Taratoo and was on his way to the airport.'

'Oh, what a nuisance,' Sister Vincent tutted. 'I really need to know the truth of this matter.'

'What matter is that, Sister?' Sister Legori wanted to know.

'Oh, just a . . . It will have to wait, I suppose.' Sister Vincent was flustered. She didn't want the kitchen nuns upset, but I suppose being a nun she couldn't directly tell a lie.

'Maybe you could catch him at the airport,' I suggested.

'I have a school to run, I can't be racing to airports,' Sister Vincent said, in even more of a fluster. 'But I really don't want to have to wait till spring to sort out this matter.'

'What matter?' Sister Legori asked again.

'Oh, it's just—' Sister Vincent was saved from lying by me having a brilliant idea.

'Sister, if you've no time to be going to airports, maybe you could go up to the farm and see if George's brother has a phone number or an address for him in Spain?'

'Excellent!' Sister Vincent boomed. 'What a thoroughly tremendous idea.'

'Oh, surely he will have a number,' Sister Finton said.

Sister Legori looked a bit suspicious. All her beard hairs seemed to be standing out anxiously. 'I hope there's not a problem with George – he's been marvellous with our new puppy. Trained it almost overnight. Like a genius with animals, George is, like a genius. There isn't a problem, is there?'

'Oh, not a problem at all, Sister,' Sister Vincent said. 'We know we can always trust George.' She turned to go.

'You'll see, Sister,' Bernadette blurted out. 'What I told you is true.'

Sister Vincent looked back at her. 'Get on with helping wash up,' she said sharply. 'And don't go gossiping about this.'

As soon as she'd gone, Sister Finton sidled over and said, 'I know she said no gossiping, but surely you could tell us.'

'Yes, surely you could tell us. What did you tell her that

was true?' Sister Legori looked like a naughty garden gnome.

Bernadette looked at me, panic-stricken.

I told the best lie I could think of in a hurry, which was only half a lie. 'My dad's been lost since I was a baby. We think it might be George but he's not sure because he can't remember things.'

Sister Legori's eyes went wide. 'George?'

'Yes, maybe,' I said. 'There have to be top-secret investigations.'

'Oh yes, yes, top secret,' Bernadette said. 'Police and everything.'

'Well, my goodness,' Sister Legori said, and got on with loading the dishwasher.

'Not another word,' said Sister Finton, scraping plates. But you could see they were dying to talk to each other about it.

After a few minutes Sister Legori said, 'Children, go and finish clearing the dining-room tables, then you can go on to class.' Obviously they were in a hurry to get rid of us.

We worked fast. We were in a hurry to find Chiquita and tell her the new developments. And then we had to find Danielle to tell her that just because things had gone quiet with Sister Vincent for a while, it didn't mean she wasn't doomed.

CHAPTER SIXTEEN

We caught Danielle on her own in the locker room. She was putting away some sweets that must have arrived for her in the morning post. Tidying them in behind her towels and sports kit, so no one could see how many sweets she had stored. Typical.

'What do you idiots want?' she said as she threw the remains of the parcel on the floor of her locker and slammed the door shut.

I explained to her that George had gone to Spain but Sister Vincent was going to track him down by phone. She just stared at me. I expected she was thinking up some horrible remark about how I was a liar and had no dad.

But Bernadette butted in before Danielle could speak: 'So, Miss Show-off, you might be off the hook, but only for a few hours.'

'Maybe less,' Chiquita added.

Surprisingly, Danielle didn't have anything clever to say about no dads, or wee smells or Chiquita's mum. Her eyes filled with tears, then she put her hands over her face.

'I can't believe this. I didn't mean to kill the stupid dog. I thought it would just run around in the fields and you'd get in trouble. I wouldn't have done it if I thought it would get killed.' She started sobbing and sobbing. Through the tears she stuttered, 'Why did I do such a stupid thing? That poor dog.'

I almost felt sorry for her.

Bernadette obviously didn't. 'You'll be in such trouble,' she said spitefully. 'You've always been Sister Vincent's big favourite so when she finds out about all your lies and murderings, she'll be doubly angry that you tricked her. I expect you'll get expelled.'

Danielle looked at her, horrified. 'Expelled?'

'I bet you will,' said Bernadette.

Danielle rubbed hard under her eyes to take away the tears and said quietly, voice shaking, 'You're right. I think I could be expelled for this.'

Maybe her parents would take her up to the execution floor, axe off her head and . . . Oh no, that wasn't quite true. But she did seem to be very scared about being expelled.

Danielle kept sniffing and trying to stop crying in a pitiful way, while Bernadette went on about how if she got expelled, she'd probably have to go to a prison school for killing a dog and she'd never get any exams or get a job, and would end up having to be a criminal for life and probably die in prison . . .

When Bernadette finished talking, Danielle suddenly stopped looking pitiful. She looked at each of us in a very threatening way and snarled, 'OK, so maybe I will get expelled. But if I go, don't think I'll be leaving without some other people getting expelled too.' And she smiled a frightening insane smile and skipped off as if nothing was wrong.

Even though the minutes were ticking by until her crimes were proven by George, Danielle didn't seem to be as totally destroyed as we'd hoped. In fact, by some un-believable cheek and nerve, she seemed to have already thought up some plan to destroy us all back, big time.

Maybe, even if they didn't have stuffed people's heads on the walls, she was going to get her family to use their money and power to do something terrible to us.

Chiquita said, 'Maybe the Kirkham-Byleses will pay George millions of pounds not to tell the truth.'

'That's it, that's exactly what they'll do!' Bernadette shouted furiously.

No. I didn't believe George could be bribed to lie, even for ten billion pounds. But some terrible plan had obviously occurred to Danielle and put the smile back on her smug face.

CHAPTER SEVENTEEN

I was supposed to be listening to our class teacher, Sister Patricia, talk to us about a book we were going to start reading for English called *David Copperfield*, but I was writing a letter to my grandad.

Telling Mum about George might make her go weird and secretive. Maybe he wasn't nice before he was hit on the head but he did seem nice now. Not very exciting like a supermodel or anything, but at least a mystery in my life would be solved. So if George did turn out to be my dad, I would need Grandad's help in getting Mum to like him. To like him again.

I told Grandad everything that had happened and all the evidence so far.

Hopefully he would still remember details about my dad that might be useful clues. Was there a sister in Spain? A brother with a farm up here in Yorkshire? Did he have very dark hair and brown eyes? Hopefully Grandad wouldn't be too busy being a glamorous bodyguard for Stella Diaz to go through my questions.

'Katherine Milne, you can start reading chapter one,' I suddenly heard Sister Patricia say. I had been writing my letter inside my exercise book to look like I was taking notes, but maybe she'd got suspicious. She was coming towards me – at any minute her frighteningly huge chest would be level with my eyes.

I quickly shut the exercise book and started to read chapter one . . .

Sister Patricia and her bosoms turned and went to the front of the classroom. I read out loud but the words didn't seem to make any sense to me. Firstly, the inside of my head was jumbled up with other thoughts, and secondly, it seemed quite a complicated book. We'd never read books with such long words at my old school. But maybe the nuns wanted to show our parents that they'd made us into geniuses overnight, because our parents paid so much money for us to go to the school.

After a while Sister Patricia asked Indira to read . . . I didn't listen. I was watching Sister Vincent out of the window. She rushed out of the side door, got into the nuns' little yellow car and drove very fast – all the nuns drove like maniacs – up the drive. I watched until I saw the car rushing up the hill on the road to the farm. Good. Time was ticking by for Danielle . . .

Or was it? What was Danielle's new sneakfest of an evil plan?

Sister Vincent was gone a long time. Maybe she was phoning Spain from the farm. Maybe the brother wouldn't help and she had to argue . . .

Loads of girls had read aloud from *David Copperfield* by the time Sister Vincent came back, driving and parking like a maniac. Had she already phoned? Was she rushing back in a rage ready to strangle Danielle with the elastic from her elasticated action veil? I waited for the classroom door to burst open.

But it didn't.

Time went by. The English lesson was over and still nothing had happened to Danielle. Then there was hockey. Which I hated. It was freezing cold, I was always shouted at by Bernadette for being useless – she was great at hockey and got completely carried away like she was the hockey boss of the universe.

Anyway . . .

Sister Vincent came running onto the pitch in her trainers, with her elasticated action veil on her head, not held out ready for strangling with. She looked irritated but she didn't say anything to Danielle. She just kept blowing her whistle and shouting hockey instructions.

Danielle, who usually did a lot of running up and down and shouting, 'Over here! To me, to me!' was very quiet. She hardly ran at all.

At one point she didn't see the ball coming right past her and Sister Vincent shouted crossly, 'Wake up, Danielle!'

Hopefully she'd be shouting more than that at Danielle soon. No wonder Danielle was playing badly: she had a lot to worry about.

Or maybe Danielle wasn't worrying. Maybe she was daydreaming about her plot to get me, Bernadette and Chiquita expelled as well. Expelled, with our heads stuffed with cotton wool, hanging on her castle walls . . .

After hockey I remembered I had to go back to the classroom to get my letter to post. Out of the window I could see Toby's van in the car park. He was supposed to be going away and not coming back until it was time to film the Christmas concert. I thought he'd probably called in to say goodbye to Danielle, but he seemed to be arguing with her. Telling her off.

Had she confessed to him about the dog? Whatever it was, she was very upset – she shouted something and came running back towards the building in tears. I ducked down under my desk in case she saw me nosing.

Next thing I knew, the classroom door flew open and Danielle stamped up to her desk. She was bound to see me because she sat behind me. She was in a real state, sobbing and muttering to herself, 'That cow, that little cow.'

There was nothing else to do but jump up and say, 'Do you mean me?'

Danielle shrieked and jumped back. When she'd got over the shock, she screamed at me like a little kid, 'I hate you!' and ran out of the classroom howling.

So I guessed she did mean me.

When I told Bernadette and Chiquita, they were hugging themselves they were so delighted that Danielle had been upset about something. But it seems that in life, and particularly in boarding-school life, just when you think there's something to be pleased about, something else spoils it.

The kitchen nuns, who were normally so friendly to us, were very grumpy when we went in to help after lunch. They made us do loads of the horrible work, washing floors and even cleaning out the dustbins. And they kept whispering to each other and looking at me.

Suddenly Sister Legori said, 'You're a very bad girl, Katie, telling those stories about George.'

I stared at her. 'What stories, Sister?'

'We decided we had to know the whole story so we asked Sister Vincent. She said she was doing no such thing as phoning to see if George is your father. You're a very bad girl and your friends are no better. When you've finished there, we don't want you helping in this kitchen any more. Sister Vincent can find you some other punishment.'

Sister Finton was beside her and just kept nodding and making cross grunty noises.

I was so upset I didn't know what to do.

Bernadette pleaded, 'But, Sister Legori—'

'No, Bernadette, we've had a lot of upset lately and you've all just added to it. I suppose you thought you were very clever, making fun of us with your stories, Katie, but it was just bad of you.'

Sister Finton stopped nodding and looked at me, sad and hurt, as if she'd just caught me drowning Taratoo or something. Then Sister Legori folded her arms and spoke in a very spiteful way: 'Sister Vincent wants to see you in her office when you're done here, Katie. And as far as we're concerned, you are done. You are to get out of the kitchen now and stay out.'

'Yes, stay out,' Sister Finton said quietly.

I glanced back at them as we walked heavy footed out of the kitchen. Sister Finton was holding onto Sister Legori's arm. They both looked so small and forlorn. Little beardy goblins alone in the world.

'This is so unfair,' Bernadette said out in the corridor. 'Go back and tell them the whole truth.'

'I can't,' I said. 'They're upset enough.'

My grandad had lots of sayings. One of his favourites was: if you make a mistake, don't make the mistake of not putting the mistake right at the first opportunity. It wasn't catchy or slick but if you stuck by it, it usually sorted your life out a bit.

I told Bernadette to go off, find Chiquita and Indira and enjoy themselves persecuting Danielle until they found out what had upset her. I was going straight to Sister Vincent on my own and I'd just explain everything sensibly.

'If you're sure you don't want me to come with you?' Bernadette asked.

'It's me she wants,' I said. And Bernadette nodded, then ran off up the corridor.

I knocked on the office door, taking a deep breath to help me be brave and sensible.

Sister Vincent roared, 'Enter!

'Oh yes, you, child,' she said when I came in. 'What is wrong with you that you have to cause so much trouble? Any ideas?'

I said I had no idea but I had lied to Sister Finton and Sister Legori so they wouldn't hear she was phoning Spain because Danielle was suspected of letting their dog out and getting it killed.

Sister Vincent nodded. 'Yes, yes, I understand that but why make up this bonkers tale about George being your lost father?'

'Because it's not a tale,' I said. 'It might be true.'

I talked and talked, giving her all my evidence.

While I was talking, she rummaged in her pockets. I thought she might be looking for a pen to take notes but she pulled out a whistle. When I'd got to the dark-hair-and-eyes evidence, she blew the whistle.

She blew hard, then she bellowed, 'Stop, child!'

'What?' I said, a bit deaf from the whistle.

'I have quite enough to deal with running this school without this kind of imagined nonsense. No wonder the last headmistress ended up in a home. I want to hear no more about this. The kitchen Sisters are extremely upset.'

'But I didn't tell them to make fun of them. I told them to protect their feelings.'

'I know, I know, but you could have said something halfway sensible to cover up. Or said nothing.' She sighed. 'Well, what's done is done, there's no point telling the poor kitchen Sisters the truth, or another story to upset them. Just leave them alone, do you hear me?'

I nodded. I could just about still hear.

'Now go away and behave yourself. You've got out of helping in the kitchen but I can find other punishments if there's bad behaviour. A run around the hockey pitch wouldn't be very nice first thing in the morning, would it?'

'No, Sister.'

'Well, that's what could happen. Go away now, Katherine, and behave yourself.'

'But, Sister . . .' I was so desperate to know if she'd phoned Spain, I had to ask. 'What about George?'

'Apparently George won't arrive at his sister's for at least another three hours, so go to your lessons and leave me to run the school, if you don't mind.'

As I was heading for the door, she must have been thinking about my problems. She suddenly called me back. 'Katie,' she said, 'why don't you ask your mother about your father instead of deciding everyone is your father?'

'I don't decide everyone—' I started to argue. Then I

shrugged and said, 'She doesn't talk about it. Grandad says she's still angry at him for going off.'

'Yes, but this idea about George . . . You can't go telling a story like that. It's embarrassing for all concerned.'

'But it could be true.'

Sister Vincent sighed and smiled her kindest kind-horse smile. 'Frankly, dear, it seems most unlikely to me. And George is far away for the next couple of months. So I think you should be sensible and try and talk to your mother about all this in the Christmas holidays.'

Maybe it would be sensible, but Sister Vincent had no idea how bonkers my mum went if you talked about my dad.

Besides, as my grandad once told me, it hurt her feelings. It made her feel like I didn't think she was good enough on her own . . . But surely, I was eleven now and it was time the whole thing stopped being a big secret.

I came out of Sister Vincent's office feeling very down and confused, but waiting at the end of the corridor was good news.

Indira was with Chiquita and Bernadette. She had overheard Danielle on the phone to Toby in the lunch break, begging and crying on her secret mobile. 'She was crying about the documentary. She kept saying, "But they can't cut me out, they can't."'

This must be the same reason she was crying all over Toby in the morning. Was she being cut out of the documentary? I really hoped so, but it would be so disappointing if we'd misunderstood.

There was only one way to find out. We had about five minutes before lessons started and we tracked Danielle down. She was sitting on her own in the locker room, eating sweets and looking like she'd just finished crying.

'What do you creeps want?' she snapped at us, and stood up as if she was going to walk away.

'How come you're going to be cut out of the documentary then?' Bernadette asked straight out.

Danielle stared at her as if she'd like to stuff her head. Then she pointed viciously at Chiquita. 'Toby's stupid boss thinks this boring cow is more interesting than me. They're going to cut loads with me in it and re-film my bits with her instead. But they'll have to film the concert and you're not in that. So I'll probably get discovered and be a star in my own right, not just because I'm the daughter of a model who everyone knows is past it now anyway.'

Then she walked off, leaving Chiquita crying, Indira shocked and Bernadette about to explode with rage.

'Don't worry about her,' I said. 'She won't be a star. She'll be expelled.'

Chiquita, still crying, ran off to be upset on her own somewhere, so we couldn't try and cheer her up by talking more about Danielle being expelled.

'She is bound to be expelled, isn't she?' Indira said. 'I

mean, if I was headmistress, I wouldn't keep a girl of such obvious bad character.'

But what seemed obvious to normal people wasn't always obvious to nuns. Also, there was still that rumbling fear that Danielle had a plan to get us and destroy us.

As it turned out, she did get us, but not in the way we expected.

CHAPTER EIGHTEEN

Danielle wasn't expelled. George had given his evidence and everything but it wasn't enough to get her expelled. For me, that was almost as bad as being taken to the execution floor for stuffing.

Bernadette reckoned it was because Danielle's incredibly rich parents had paid for the new computers this term, and had probably promised to pay for something else next term. And because Toby had promised to give half the money from the documentary to nuns looking after lepers in India.

Or maybe she'd just cried and said she didn't mean to kill the dog so convincingly that Sister Vincent had forgiven her. Whatever. We were stuck with her.

Indira said that a big public fuss might mean the truth about Tara would get back to the kitchen nuns, and nobody wanted that. They were happy now with their new puppy. I saw them going out for walks and I missed them a lot. Them hating me was really Danielle's fault – it was another way she'd got me.

Nothing was said in public, but Sister Vincent made an announcement in our class study. She said Danielle had decided not to take part in the Christmas concert and her place would be given to Indira.

So that was obviously her punishment: no concert. And I suppose it was also a punishment that she couldn't be Sister Vincent's favourite any more. But you never knew with Danielle. She was so sneaky, she was bound to find some way to get herself Queen of Everything again.

For the time being, though, she did seem very mopey and just went around saying she had hurt her voice and the doctor had told her she couldn't sing for six months. Some idiots seemed to believe her.

I felt mopey because I'd had a long letter from Grandad that made me feel I'd been pathetic and over-imagining about George.

In the letter was a photograph of my mum's wedding. My dad was a small blond man who didn't look remotely like George.

'We'd been keeping the photos to show you when you were older but I suppose you are older now,' he said. 'I had this one in my belongings so I didn't bother telling your mum that you'd been asking – you know how she gets ...'

Then he went on about how he'd been in Paris and Madrid at fashion shows and didn't sound like my proper grandad at all. I didn't want to hear about these foreign places. I wanted him to realize that I was getting sick of having a run-off dad. I wanted him to give me some wise advice. Or use all the detecting he knew to find where my real dad had gone once and for all.

Bernadette had a letter too. She was going to Hong Kong for Christmas and her parents were asking her what presents she'd like.

Indira had a letter saying her parents were coming to the Christmas concert and they'd all be together in England for the Christmas holidays.

Chiquita didn't have a letter talking about lovely family Christmas blah blah things but she was in a very happy mood because Toby was back and wanted to film her doing the things Danielle had done – explaining about the school and so on. This wasn't just good news for Chiquita. Because Chiquita wasn't very good at talking, they asked me, Bernadette and Indira to be with her, helping out with the talking. But I just felt I didn't care about all that at the moment.

I should have been excited – I was getting to be on television a lot – but I kept wondering about the small blond man in the photo. Not about some vague chance he might see me on TV in future; I was thinking about the past. Why had he just gone off like that and not cared about me and Mum? I suddenly felt really lonely and wished my grandad was in his normal house where I could phone him. Maybe it was selfish but I missed the old times, when the only interesting thing in his life was me.

Grandad's wife, my grandma, had died before I was born. Grandad had depended on me and Mum to keep him company, stop him feeling too sad and go for pizza and such things. It was only fair that, if he had a chance now, he should go adventuring. It wasn't his job to look after me – it was my dad's.

I went out for a walk around the gardens with Chiquita, even though it was freezing cold and she was complaining about that all the way. Everyone else was playing in the hall. I thought if I talked to her, I'd feel better. For most of her life Chiquita thought she had no parents at all, so she'd understand why I was worrying about my dad. Maybe this was a subject on which she'd have some wise ideas. But before I started telling her all my jumbled-up feelings, we were distracted.

A very fancy car came up the drive and parked by the school entrance. A woman got out, then a man got out of the driver's seat. It was Stella Diaz and my grandad.

CHAPTER NINETEEN

Stella and Chiquita ran towards each other and started hugging and crying in a very dramatic way. Grandad just came up and hugged me in a calm sort of way, without crying.

I asked the obvious question: 'What are you doing here?'

'Well,' he said, looking awkward, 'first of all I was a bit worried about you after your letter, and then all this fuss started with Stella so we decided we'd both come here as soon as we could and sort it out.'

I was going to ask him what the fuss was, but then I realized Stella and Chiquita weren't hugging any more.

Stella was looking all exasperated and saying, 'But why, sweetheart, why?'

'Why what?' I asked Grandad.

'I don't know,' he said. 'Stella's had all these phone calls from a television company wanting to interview her about Chiquita and they said they'd been filming Chiquita. And the cheeky beggars even claimed they had permission. I mean, if Stella had given her permission, she'd have remembered, wouldn't she?'

Stella came over, holding Chiquita by the hand. She looked a bit stressed but not really angry. 'It seems somebody signed the permission letter for me,' she said.

Chiquita looked very ashamed of herself. 'I wanted it to be a surprise,' she muttered.

'But, sweetheart . . .' Stella sighed. 'Oh, it's not your fault, you don't know how these people are with celebrities. But I wanted our life to be private. Now I'll have to answer all kinds of questions about you, give interviews . . .'

Chiquita looked upset but Grandad saved the day by saying, 'The thing is, Stella, they'd have found out sooner or later, so this way you can do the documentary and tell the story how you want, then tell the rest of the media and newspapers to go away.' Then he laughed. 'And I'll make sure they go away.'

Stella nodded. 'You're right, Sam,' she said.

I was a bit thrown by that: I always forgot my grandad had a name other than 'Grandad'. But then he didn't look like Grandad any more. More like a news reader or someone. Old but dressed modern, in a black suit and a very expensive-looking beige coat. I mean, he only had a horrible old blue anorak before. With some dandruff on the collar. Now he had an almost trendy haircut. I had an amazed feeling that he even had some gel in his hair.

I felt it wasn't fair if I didn't say something. 'It was me

who first told the cameraman who Chiquita was. So we could be in the documentary as much as Danielle.'

'But I told Katie it was a good idea,' Chiquita said loyally.

Stella looked at us and sighed. 'What funny little girls you are. But never mind. What's done is done. Let's find Sister Vincent and sort things out.' She smiled at Grandad. 'I'll see you later, Sam.' She led Chiquita off towards the main door of the school.

Grandad smiled at me. 'So what about you, Katie? Are you any happier?'

I said I was OK; it was just the business with George that had been confusing.

'But honest, love, you've got this all wrong. Your dad wasn't a trainee doctor. He was a postman.'

I nodded.

'I wonder,' said Grandad, 'if all this business about Chiquita and Stella has made you hope your dad might be some great person too? But honest, love, the sad truth is . . . me and your mum are all there is.'

'I don't want someone great,' I argued. 'Just someone.'

Grandad looked very sad. 'I know, love. I know.'

Maybe he did know how I felt, but it didn't make me feel better. He obviously couldn't think of anything more helpful because he changed the subject. 'So what about this Danielle and the dog? Stella says Chiquita has been writing pages and pages about that girl. Surely she should be sent home?'

I explained about how she'd got away with it, and Grandad listened carefully, shaking his head and tutting occasionally.

In some ways it wasn't a change of subject for me. Danielle was to blame for the dad business. I really wanted to have someone to show her and say, 'See, look, a dad, so stop saying all that disgusting stuff about my mum having lots of boyfriends and not knowing who my dad is.'

We went for a walk around the grounds in the cold. I took Grandad down to the little place under the trees where Tara was buried. Sister Finton and Sister Legori were standing there with Taratoo on her lead.

They nodded and looked as though they were going to scurry away.

'This is my grandad,' I said.

The nuns were polite as he introduced himself to them. Then he asked, 'Now are those County Wexford accents . . . ?'

And the nuns giggled. Next thing I knew they were talking on and on like old friends about some place in Ireland. All ignoring me – and Taratoo, who lay down and fell asleep.

My grandad had a slight Irish accent but when he started nattering with the nuns, his accent got as strong as theirs, so I only understood half of what they were saying. All about this shop and that shop, and some person from another shop who'd won the lottery and gone to Fiji . . .

I started stroking Taratoo, thinking how nice it would be to teach her tricks, when I heard Grandad saying, 'So isn't it terrible about that Danielle one letting out your old dog?'

And before I could stop him he'd told the kitchen nuns the whole story about Danielle and why they hadn't been told to protect their feelings . . .

I expected them to run around the trees crying and going crazy but they just stared at Grandad.

'Well, for goodness' sake,' Sister Legori said. 'We'd far rather have been told the truth.'

'George thought you shouldn't be told,' I explained. 'He thought you were upset enough.'

'Yes, we were upset, but even so,' Sister Legori said, 'we're not stupid.'

'That's what I thought as soon as I started talking to you,' said Grandad. 'You see, Sisters, it's because we're old, people always think we must be idiots.'

The kitchen nuns nodded.

'Well, Katie,' said Sister Legori, 'next time, try and think like your grandad and just tell people the truth even if they are old. And when we see that George again, we'll tell him the same thing.'

Then Sister Finton started talking about how cold it was and asked me and Grandad up to the kitchen for tea and chocolate biscuits.

Grandad had turned up and been wise. I could still

count on him. Even if he was wearing a flash suit and hair gel. Suddenly I felt cheerful again. I wasn't alone in the world with my troubles after all.

CHAPTER TWENTY

Chiquita and me were sad when her mum went off again with Grandad. They had to go to some fashion thing in Canada somewhere. We'd see them again at the Christmas concert but that was still a few weeks away.

Bernadette came out into the garden to look for us. Her little eyes went as wide as they could when she heard it all.

'So your mum must be so furious with you, Chiquita.'

'Not really. Considering I'd been telling lies and I'd forged her signature on the permission letter. She just said she was disappointed in me.'

'Huh,' Bernadette grunted. 'Parents always say "disappointed" when they're really furious.'

'She wasn't furious.' Chiquita almost stamped her foot. I don't know why Bernadette had said such a horrible thing. Perhaps she was jealous because she hadn't had any visitors. To stop an argument I asked Chiquita what had happened when they went in to see Sister Vincent.

'Nothing much. My mum said the documentary was OK but no more press were to be allowed. She told Sister Vincent she has to be careful people from the newspapers don't come up to the school and start hassling me and taking pictures. And Sister Vincent said, "Newspapers? If any of those scoundrels turn up here, I'll turn the fire hoses on them."'

I laughed. I could just imagine Sister Vincent saying that.

'I hope they do turn up' – Chiquita grinned – 'just to see Sister Vincent hosing them.'

'She couldn't really,' Bernadette said. 'The fire hoses are far too big for a nun on her own to squirt at people.'

'No, they're not.' Chiquita's grin disappeared into a frown. 'I saw Sister Ita using one when the dustbins caught fire last summer.'

'I bet there were other people in the shed helping.' Bernadette scowled.

Chiquita looked as though she might start crying. She did this sometimes if people disagreed with her.

To solve the completely unnecessary argument I said we should look at the fire hoses and see how many people it would take to squirt them.

Bernadette led the way to a shed near the car park.

'Wait till you see,' Chiquita said. 'Bernadette is completely wrong.'

Bernadette made a growling sound and walked faster.

I'd noticed the shed before, but I thought it was for gardening stuff. The door handle was very stiff. Bernadette struggled with it, muttering, 'See, even the handle's too heavy for one person.'

'You're doing that on purpose,' Chiquita muttered back.

'It's really hurting my hands, stupid,' Bernadette said as she opened the door.

Underneath all this bickering, they were good friends, I promise you . . .

Inside the shed were four huge hosepipes attached to great big stands. On top of the stands were levers marked ON/OFF.

Just for something to do, we unravelled one of the hoses, and Bernadette said, 'The water comes out in a really big fast jet so we'd better not turn them on.'

'How can we show you're wrong if we don't turn them on?' Chiquita snapped.

'I wish Danielle would come past and we could squirt her,' I said, to make them laugh and stop the argument starting again.

But instead, a van pulled up and parked just by the door. Clive the cameraman was inside. He got out, talking angrily on his mobile phone.

'I'm outside the school now, Toby, and I'm telling them if you don't agree to give me half the money . . .'

We kept very still, listening.

'No, a quarter isn't enough. Come on, Toby. If I tell

them, they'll tell the bosses and you'll be finished, so don't keep refusing . . .'

This sounded very interesting. Something that could get Toby in trouble. If her brother was disgraced, it was almost as good as getting Danielle in trouble. I could see that Chiquita and Bernadette felt like me, hardly daring to breathe in case Clive heard us.

Suddenly he sounded less cross. 'OK, Toby, I thought you'd see sense.' Then he laughed. 'I'll go home then.'

He started walking back towards his van. I panicked: he was going to leave and we'd never find out what he was up to – it was obviously something bad . . . Holding one of the big hoses, I pushed my way out of the shed.

I pointed the nozzle at Clive and shouted, 'Stop or I'll fire!'

He stared at me and then started laughing. I realized I looked pretty stupid, but then he'd be laughing on the other side of his face if he got a jet of water up his nose.

'What are you kids up to now?' he asked in a patronizing way.

'Listening to you,' I said. 'And we want to know what you're up to.'

'Or what, you'll squirt me with a hose?' Clive laughed a bit more and started walking back to his van.

'Chiquita, the lever!' I shouted.

Chiquita must have acted fast to switch the water on. The hose suddenly got really heavy and jumped out of my control. Bernadette had to leap forward and help me. Maybe she'd been right – Chiquita couldn't have seen one nun controlling the hose. We really struggled to keep hold of it as a huge jet of water blasted Clive in the back.

'Yow!' he yelled. He looked back and then ran. We kept squirting the water in his direction, although it was nearly impossible to keep a grip on the hose.

Water was going everywhere, some of it on Clive, who was letting out a stream of swearing like . . . like water from a hose.

He got into his van, started the engine and reversed really fast. I tried to squirt the windscreen but the hose had a life of its own. It was no use, Clive had escaped.

I turned round to tell Chiquita to turn the water off when I saw Sister Vincent coming out of the kitchen door. I saw her and then I saw her covered in water. It hit the top of her head, swooshing off her veil – unfortunately not her elasticated action veil. Or fortunately, because that might have pinged right back and smacked her head with wet veil.

We struggled to turn the water jet away from Sister Vincent.

'Turn it off!' I screamed at Chiquita.

She did, but it was too late. A big wet nun in a state of shock was standing there, shivering with fright and freezing cold.

'Sorry, Sister,' I said.

Sister Vincent was so shocked it seemed to take her a

while to remember how to speak. So she just shivered and dripped for a moment.

Then she bellowed at me, 'What do you think you are doing?!'

I thought of pretending I'd seen a fire but then realized this was a rubbish excuse.

'I was trying to squirt Clive the cameraman, who's up to something,' I said.

'What?' Sister Vincent shivered and stared at me. Her short grey hair was all flattened to her head with water.

I didn't know what else to tell her to defend ourselves, because we didn't exactly know what Clive was up to.

Chiquita was coming out of the shed behind us. 'Oh dear,' she said when she saw the state of Sister Vincent.

'Never mind "oh dear".' Sister Vincent's voice was trembling with rage or cold, or both. 'Attempt to explain this behaviour to me again!'

'We were hosing Clive, Sister,' Bernadette said. 'We overheard him on the phone – he's up to no good.'

Sister Vincent waved a hand as if batting away what Bernadette had said. 'Never mind what other people are up to, what are you three doing in the fire shed?'

There wasn't much we could say about that. 'We just wanted to check everything was in order, Sister,' I tried.

'The fire shed is none of your business, you ridiculous child!' she roared at me. 'And what is the matter with you anyway? Why are you always doing something? These other two children were no trouble at all before you came. You are some kind of fiend. I honestly believe that now – you are a fiend child sent to torment me!'

'Sorry, Sister,' I said, although I didn't think I was a fiend.

'Put that hose away and go and play in the hall with the other children while I decide what is to be done about you.' She picked up her sopping wet veil and hurried back indoors, hugging her arms around herself to keep warm.

I picked up the hose and dragged it back into the shed. Bernadette found a lever that said REWIND so we didn't have to put the hose back by hand. A mechanism rattled it back around the stand.

Bernadette, like me, was stunned into silence at what had happened.

In a couldn't-care-less way, Chiquita said, 'Well, that's it then. It'll be us that gets expelled.'

'Oh, that's disgustingly not fair!' Bernadette shrieked.

Chiquita looked surprised that Bernadette was shrieking. 'I thought you were leaving soon anyway, if your parents are coming to live in London?'

'What do you mean "if"?' I could see Bernadette was going to fight her at any minute.

'So it's no big deal then,' Chiquita said. 'If I get expelled, I can be with my mother all the time. We were planning for that next term anyway.'

'What about Katie?' Bernadette had gone very spiky-faced

with anger. 'She doesn't want to leave like us – she just got here.'

I didn't know how I felt about being expelled. It would be good to be home, having a normal life with my mum. But it meant I would lose the huge inheritance I was supposed to get if I stayed with the nuns until I was eighteen. It would mean my mum was always going to be poor and my grandad would probably be disappointed I'd been so badly behaved . . . No, actually, it was probably better not to get expelled.

Bernadette closed up the shed again.

Chiquita sighed and said, 'Well, we might as well go to the hall.'

'Yes, let's see if we can do something else to get expelled,' Bernadette snapped at her.

Chiquita shrugged. 'Who cares?'

'I do,' Bernadette said. 'You might be so spoiled it doesn't matter what you do, but my parents will be very disappointed in me if I get expelled. I mean "disappointed" in the sense of "furious", and they probably won't even like me any more.'

How could Bernadette think such a thing? Sometimes I did wonder if it was really true that her parents were coming to live in London. They'd left her at the school for years and years and I didn't quite believe that they were going to change.

'Anyway, who says anyone will get expelled?' Chiquita

started to walk towards the main school doors. 'And I *do* care anyway because what if it gets in the documentary and disgraces my mum? Let's go in, I'm freezing.'

It was completely ice cold. Once we were warm inside we were less grumpy with each other and agreed that what we needed to do quickly was find out what Clive and Toby were doing, save the day and then we'd be off the hook.

In the hall, Danielle was sitting with her new best friend, Rachel, looking at celebrity magazines. They glared at us, then went back to looking at the pictures. I supposed Danielle had been imagining her stupid concert act would get her in the magazines. At least that wasn't going to happen now.

We went over to Indira. She was sitting all alone reading a book.

I told myself off – I had to remember to keep Indira with us at all times. Especially now that Clive had turned out to be definitely up to no good.

Actually, now I had proof he was definitely bad, I realized I should probably share the kidnap fears with the others. Now there was evidence, they'd be more likely to believe me and be careful not to wander off.

Indira put her hand over her mouth in a ladylike way and laughed and laughed when we told her about hosing Sister Vincent.

'Oh, I don't think you'll get expelled,' she said. 'Sister Vincent does have a sense of humour.'

I didn't know about that. Sister Vincent made me laugh but I'd never noticed that I made *her* laugh. What with me being a fiend and so on. We needed to get on with a plan to catch Clive and Toby urgently.

'Danielle must have Toby's number stored in that secret mobile she has,' Indira said thoughtfully. Then she shook her head. 'No, that's silly – I was going to say, Let's borrow the mobile and phone him, saying, "We know what you're up to." But what good would that do? He wouldn't be afraid of mere schoolgirls.'

Her plan wasn't that silly, though. 'What if he doesn't know it's schoolgirls? What if we pretend it's a nun calling him?' I suggested.

'Yes, yes!' Bernadette squeaked. 'You've got a really grown-up voice, Indira – you could sound like a nun. You do a scary nun's voice and say you know what he's up to, so he starts talking and from what he says you can guess what his plan is.'

Indira smiled. 'Goodness, how exciting.' She cleared her throat delicately, then did an imitation of a nun: '*Hello, this is Sister . . . Philomena.* I think Philomena's a typical nun's name, don't you? How is it sounding?'

'Excellent,' Chiquita said.

'I'd believe you were a nun, definitely,' Bernadette enthused.

'Yes, I do believe I'm getting the tone right.' Indira laughed. 'By tomorrow Sister Philomena will seem quite real. I'm rather looking forward to it.'

Before Sister Philomena made her call, Indira had to wait till Danielle fell asleep, sneak a look at the numbers in her secret mobile and then we'd call from Chiquita's secret mobile – withholding the number so we couldn't be traced.

Oh, but unfortunately, before the important, possibly skin-saving phone call, we had to be in trouble for hosing Sister Vincent.

Red-faced Sister Ita came in to take evening study, telling us that Sister Vincent was ill. Just as we all sat down, she said, 'Katherine Milne, Chiquita Diaz and Bernadette Kelly, you can stand up again, please.'

We stood and Sister Ita glared at us.

'Sister Vincent has so much work to do: she has the school to run, lessons to teach and the end-of-term concert to organize. She really doesn't need to be in bed with a nasty cold caused by you. Please tell me what you were doing in the fire-hose shed.'

'Just looking,' I said quickly, before Bernadette got some demented owning-up urge and started talking about Clive.

'You have no business "just looking". That shed is out of bounds. You three are behaving so badly this term. When Sister Vincent is well enough, she will have big decisions to make about what's to be done with you.'

That sounded like we could still be expelled. Instead of Danielle getting us with some evil plot, we'd somehow managed to get ourselves.

On the way to bed that night Danielle said with a big grin, 'You three are *so* not going to be here next term.'

We didn't say anything. Indira, walking behind Danielle, winked at us. Yes, everything would be all right. We were going to catch Toby out, disgrace the Kirkham-Byles family and save the day.

CHAPTER TWENTY-ONE

We had to be quick on the phone. As you know, we weren't supposed to have mobiles. Especially not for making fake calls when we were meant to be on our way from assembly to class.

Indira did a very good Sister Philomena voice. She said she'd overheard Clive the cameraman and knew what was going on. Then she went quiet and her face looked more and more shocked. Suddenly she said, 'But you know you won't get away with it.' She moved the phone away from her ear and made a face. Then she switched off the phone. 'Well, that was charming.'

'What? What?' all of us asked.

'Well, he said, "Look, Sister, this is none of your business and there's nothing you can do about it. And if you try and stop me, there'll be no donation to India and there'll be nothing you can do." So then I said the you-won't-get-away-with-it thing and he said, "You know I will, Sister," and hung up on me.'

'Argh,' said Bernadette. 'But we still don't know what "it" is.'

'Just goes to show he's as two-faced as Danielle,' I said. 'Acting all nice to the nuns when he's here.'

Indira frowned. 'I think it's awful that he's using that donation to poor people in India as a bribe.'

'Yes,' said Bernadette. 'If I was a nun, I'd tell him to shove his donation.'

'I wonder,' said Indira, looking like an extremely sophisticated detective, 'what his superiors at the television company would think if they knew he was using it as a bribe.'

'If only we'd taped the conversation,' I moaned. 'We could have found his boss's number and played it down the phone.'

'And we still don't know what he's up to with Clive,' Bernadette complained.

There was no more time for moaning because we heard Sister Ita's voice round the corner. 'Who's that chattering in the corridor? Why aren't you in class?'

We ran down the corridor, skidding and grabbing onto each other to keep steady, and just made it round the next corner before she saw us.

CHAPTER TWENTY-TWO

Sister Vincent had a cold but she had appeared at lunch break to get us to practise the school song for the concert. Everyone in the school who wasn't doing an individual act got on stage at the end and sang together. The school song had no tune and was full of ridiculous lyrics about how by wearing blue and white we would always do right...

Most of the rehearsal had involved organizing people in height order, with lots of shuffling around and people who had to stand on benches falling over. Sister Vincent sneezed and blew her nose often. As the chaos went on, she got more and more irritated.

At one point she looked at me and said, 'Ah yes, you. You troublesome little girl, I haven't forgotten about you.' But then luckily a Year Eleven girl fell off the stage and she had to deal with that.

After rehearsals we weren't so lucky: she told us to wait behind.

'You deserve more punishment but for the time being,

all of you are to work in the kitchen every morning and after every lunch for the rest of term.'

Then she went away. Sneezing.

So that was the unfortunate result of Grandad making friends with the kitchen nuns. Somewhere along the line they must have told Sister Vincent that they didn't think I was so bad after all. And they'd be happy to have me back doing washing-up punishments.

As before, they were very kind, giving us biscuits and sweets. They talked a lot about Grandad, telling me how wonderful he was.

Taratoo slept in her basket under the table looking very cute, but they wouldn't let us play with her or teach her tricks.

'Ah no, she's just a baby dog. As long as she knows to do her business in the back yard, that's all the tricks she needs.'

When they took her out to do her business, they put her on a lead. Obviously they were terrified of another runaway dog incident.

We tried to keep ourselves cheerful by concentrating on our detecting plans. At the end of the week Toby and Clive would be back, so we'd decided we would stalk them at all times to find out what crime they were trying to commit.

In the meantime, kitchen work, kitchen work, kitchen work . . .

*   *   *

One morning we were getting crockery from the cupboards to set up for breakfast and watching with amazement as Sister Legori made a big saucepan of beige sludge that she called 'lovely porridge'.

Bernadette was obsessed with watching her make the porridge, waiting to see if any beard bits fell in.

Poor Sister Legori thought she was interested because she liked the porridge and said, 'Today, as a treat, Bernadette, I'll let you stir the porridge.'

So Bernadette was stuck turning a big wooden spoon, making her arm tired and with no beard-watching fun.

It was nearly time for breakfast when the door opened and Sister Vincent came in.

'Morning, Sisters. Morning, girls.' She still had a cold and held a large white hanky, more the size of a pillowcase, up to her nose. 'I have been thinking about what to do with you girls for drenching me with the hose and generally behaving like fiends. I've decided that as you are so fond of water, you can wash all the school corridors in all your tea and evening break times next week. So much mud gets in at this time of year the cleaners can hardly keep up with it.'

'But, Sister . . .' I started, although I didn't really have an argument. The thing was, if all our break times were taken up with the kitchen or cleaning, how would we do our stalking?

Bernadette clearly had the same thought. 'But, Sister, we're already doing this punishment.'

'It's not enough.' Sister Vincent frowned. 'My head is splitting and I am really very cross indeed and want you to have another punishment and that's that.'

Chiquita showed she was a true model's daughter and came up with the best excuse: 'But, Sister, I'm being filmed next week and cleaning corridors will ruin my hands.'

'Then you'll be happy to wear the rubber gloves provided,' Sister Vincent said. And suddenly she held her hanky up to her face. She let out the most enormous sneeze. When she talked, it was like a foghorn, so her sneeze – well, it was like an explosion in a siren factory.

We all jumped but little Taratoo leaped halfway across the kitchen. Then, yelping and howling, she bolted out of the door and into the dining room. Although they weren't related, she'd inherited Tara's ability to take off like a rocket.

Sister Finton shrieked, little gnarled hands flying up in the air.

Sister Legori shrieked as well: 'Taratoo! Taratoo, come back!'

I was nearest the dining room, so I ran out, just in time to see Taratoo streak out of the main door and into the hall. I ran as fast as I could, shouting for Bernadette, who was much better at running.

Taratoo ran and skidded along the polished floor of the main corridor and then shot out of the front door, nearly tripping up Sister Patricia, who was coming in with the post.

I ran past Sister Patricia, shouting, 'Dog emergency!' and nearly got wedged in the doorway by her enormous bosoms.

'*Stop!*' she shrieked, but I was gone.

Taratoo ran across the gardens, her little legs going in a blur. I tried to run faster. I could hear Bernadette shouting behind me, but I couldn't wait for her. We couldn't risk another tragic dog accident . . .

Taratoo was far ahead of me. Now she was crossing the hockey pitch. Any minute now she'd be in the fields behind the school, maybe trampled by cows, eaten by farm dogs . . .

I got splinters in my hands climbing over the wooden fence at the far side of the hockey pitch. I couldn't believe Taratoo was still running and yelping. She was racing towards a clump of apple trees where a man was up a ladder hanging some Christmas lights.

Oh no . . .

Taratoo scooted past the ladder, barking, startling the man, who was all lopsided because of holding the lights. He yelled and fell off the ladder, bringing the string of outdoor lights down with him.

Maybe realizing she'd caused an accident and was sorry, Taratoo stopped and looked at the man. I crept over, grabbed her and shoved her under my jumper, where she wriggled around but couldn't get out.

The man was lying on the wet ground, confused and holding his leg. 'What's going on?' he said, with a wince, because his leg must be hurting. Actually he swore a bit as well, but it's probably better if I don't tell you the swearing.

'I'm so sorry,' I said. 'But I had to catch the nuns' new dog.'

'The puppy?'

'I've got it now.'

'It can run as fast as old Tara, eh?'

I realized who the man must be. 'Are you George's brother?'

'Geoff. That's right.'

'I'm sorry but I had to get the dog. I hope your lights aren't broken.'

'That's OK. My wife always says outdoor Christmas lights are a bit over the top anyway.' Geoff tried to stand up and sat down again. 'Oh dear. I think I've seriously hurt my leg. There's no one in at my house right now. Can you run back to school and get someone to call an ambulance?'

'An ambulance, really?'

'Yes, I think so,' he said. He had a nice quiet voice and was a bit older than George but he looked like him.

I could see Bernadette running across the hockey pitch. I yelled at her to call an ambulance but she just stopped running and shouted, 'What?'

'I'll go myself,' I said to Geoff, who nodded and winced again in pain.

I walked very fast but I couldn't possibly run all the way back to school. I had no breath left, and although I didn't need an ambulance for my legs, they were aching like mad.

I met Bernadette at the fence. 'Run back,' I said. 'Get an ambulance for Geoff the farmer.'

'Did you get Taratoo?'

'Yes, she's here.' I showed the puppy's head but clung on to her tightly.

Bernadette ran off fast. I climbed the fence very carefully so Taratoo wouldn't escape. She was panting and had to be exhausted now, but I couldn't take the risk.

I could see Bernadette meet up with the nuns on the edge of the gardens. Sister Vincent rushed into the school with Bernadette but Sister Finton and Sister Legori waited for me.

'You got her, dear?' asked Sister Finton, her little beardy face all frightened.

'Yes, she's fine.'

I proudly lifted the little puppy out of my jumper and handed her to Sister Finton. 'Hold tight.'

'Oh, God bless you for a good child.'

They both fussed over Taratoo for a moment. Taratoo seemed bored and fell asleep.

'So what happened?' Sister Finton asked. 'Geoff fell out of a tree?'

'He thinks he's broken his leg or something,' I explained.

'Oh dear. Poor Geoff,' said Sister Finton. 'Why was he up a tree anyway?'

'He was putting up Christmas lights,' I told her.

'Oh, they do always look pretty,' Sister Legori said, stroking Taratoo's head. 'Well, come along, you must have some hot cocoa in the kitchen and this little one better have a rest. Goodness, Finton, we'll have to be so careful from now on.'

They stroked Taratoo and clucked like mother hens over her. Although she was a dog, but you see what I mean . . .

Anyway, when we arrived back, all the girls were sitting down to breakfast in the dining room.

Danielle looked up and asked gloatily, obviously expecting me to be in trouble, 'What have you done now?'

'Saved the new dog.' I grinned. 'And probably saved the farmer as well. I expect Sister Vincent will be crazy about me now.'

Danielle made a face, pretending she wasn't the least bit interested. But I was sure her insides must be twisting up with jealousy.

Sister Vincent wasn't exactly crazy about me but she let us off the corridor washing. Although she also said, 'Some might say I was being a bit soft because, if you think about it, my having a cold was your fault, so the animal running off was your fault.'

Then she sneezed again, loud enough to scare lions, let alone small puppies.

CHAPTER TWENTY-THREE

As you can probably guess, it was going to be a bit awkward and slightly scary when Clive the cameraman came back with Toby. I'd explained to the others why Clive could be a dangerous kidnapper and we'd decided there was nothing we could do except stick together at all times and hope he didn't try and grab one of us and murder us.

When he was filming, Clive looked at us like he was thinking bad things all the time. He was mainly filming us explaining about the end-of-term concert. As Chiquita couldn't think of much to say, me and Bernadette did most of the talking. I wanted Indira to be involved but Bernadette pointed out that if she was interviewed a lot, Toby might recognize her voice. So Indira just hung around quietly while we were filmed. Bernadette told me the filming was getting annoying but I was very pleased that I was going to be on television so much. Even though there was always that slight possibility of being murdered by the cameraman.

I decided we should take drastic action to find out what was going on. We knew that Toby and Clive were staying in a hotel in the town that was miles from the school. We needed to get into their hotel rooms and search through their belongings for clues and evidence.

'But as you say,' Indira pointed out, 'their hotel is miles from the school.'

I'd thought of that. 'I've thought of that,' I said.

Indira, Chiquita and Bernadette all looked at me as if they didn't believe me. They forgot how much I knew about detective matters.

'It's easy,' I said. 'When they've finished filming, we hide in the back of the van. Then we creep out after they've driven to the hotel, then creep into their rooms.'

I expected my friends look more impressed.

'Keys?' Bernadette asked, looking very know-all.

'Oh yes.' Chiquita frowned. 'What about keys?'

Honestly, didn't any of them ever watch detective programmes?

Patiently I explained it to them. 'We tell the woman cleaning the rooms that they are dangerous men and she'll lend us her keys.'

Indira looked doubtful. 'Will she?'

Bernadette snorted. 'Of course she won't. And, anyway, I'm not sneaking out of school. We'd get in so much trouble – and it's not as if we need more of that.'

Chiquita said she agreed with Bernadette. I was really

furious with them. How could they be so negative and pathetic?

'You're useless,' I said. 'And cowards.'

Bernadette grabbed my arm, giving me a Chinese burn. 'Take that back!' she shouted.

'No!' I shouted, mainly shouting because the Chinese burn really hurt.

We were so busy fighting and making a noise we didn't see that Clive had come into the classroom. He stood in the doorway so we couldn't escape. He'd trapped us.

The only thing I could think of doing was screaming at him: 'Don't do anything or we'll jump out of the windows!'

'Will we?' Chiquita looked worried.

Sometimes Chiquita was just hopeless.

Bernadette cleverly opened her desk and shouted, 'And I've got a knife in here!' Although she only had a can of Coke.

Clive just smiled. 'What is the matter with you kids? Why are you acting so terrified of me?'

'We know what you're up to,' I said, opening a desk, trying the pretending-I-might-have-a-knife thing too.

'And what's that then?' Clive smirked and leaned across the doorway.

'You're up to something with Toby,' I said.

He just kept smirking. 'It's nothing for you kids to worry about.'

'It's not just us kids, it's the nuns as well,' I lied

frantically. 'They've told us to investigate.'

Clive laughed. 'Is that right?' Then he turned to leave the classroom. 'Oh, by the way, Toby and I have been looking for a nun called Sister Philomena. Have you ever heard of her?'

'Of course,' I said quickly.

'That's funny.' Clive smirked. 'Toby asked Sister Vincent if he could meet her and she said there was no Sister Philomena here.'

'She's away,' I said.

'In India,' Indira added.

'Oh right,' Clive said in a sarcastic way. 'Well, in that case I'll leave you to your investigations.'

Then he went out.

I realized that everything I'd said had been pretty dumb. He could see we were just kids making up knives and instructions from nuns. And somehow they'd guessed that Sister Philomena wasn't real.

'We should have grabbed him and tortured him until he told,' said Bernadette, slamming down her desk lid angrily.

'I wonder how they knew about Sister Philomena,' Indira said. 'I really thought I was most convincing.'

'All they had to do was ask Danielle. She'd have said "Never heard of her." I bet they didn't even really have to check with Sister Vincent,' Bernadette muttered.

'Yes, I see that now.' Indira sighed. 'It wasn't really a very good idea, was it?'

'It would have been a good idea if they'd told Sister Philomena what they were up to,' I pointed out.

'Yes, yes,' Indira said. 'It's just unfortunate that all the Sister Philomena plan achieved was to let them know we were suspicious and make us look foolish.'

'So now we have to follow them to the hotel,' I said. 'We have to stop them laughing at us.'

'No way.' Chiquita shook her head. 'Definitely no way. Too scary.'

Bernadette and Indira said they wouldn't go to the hotel but would do any other plans I had that wouldn't involve expelled-level trouble.

Unfortunately, I didn't have any plans like that.

CHAPTER TWENTY-FOUR

After filming us showing the Christmas tree the nuns had put up in the dining room, Toby suddenly said, 'So which one of you is Sister Philomena?'

'I don't know what you're talking about,' Bernadette said quickly.

Toby laughed. 'You know I checked up on her. Because the more I thought about it, the more the voice on the phone struck me as belonging to someone quite young. Someone about eleven years old.'

Clive grinned. 'Eleven years old like these kids, you mean?'

Toby laughed again. 'These are smart kids, though. I think they and their friend Sister Philomena will just leave us alone now, or who knows what could happen? One of your valuable pieces of camera equipment, or my mobile phone or something could turn up in their belongings and the nuns would never believe anything a thief told them.'

I could see he was definitely Danielle's brother. This was a trick exactly like tricks she'd done.

'Don't worry,' I said. 'We won't say anything.'

'Now that *is* smart,' Toby said, and went off with Clive.

I was excited. Finally I had a plan. I would take Toby's own idea and turn it round on him. We'd steal something valuable belonging to the nuns and put it in their van.

'But that's still stealing.' Bernadette looked worried.

'What would we steal that would be valuable?' Chiquita said. Then she looked excited. 'I know: Taratoo.'

'Don't be disgusting,' Bernadette said.

I agreed. 'That's too upsetting for the kitchen nuns.'

Then I had a thought about how to improve my idea. Something would go missing that the nuns would notice very quickly, even if they didn't think it was valuable . . .

'That's too dangerous,' Chiquita said.

'I agree,' said Bernadette.

I was a bit scared but it was too good an idea to abandon it.

I told them that their first job was to get Indira involved, because in dealing with the nuns she came across as sensible and believable, whereas Chiquita and Bernadette were still a bit in the fiend area . . .

What was the plan?

Basically what I was going to do was kidnap myself.

CHAPTER TWENTY-FIVE

It is much harder to kidnap yourself than you might think.

First of all you need to get your friends to help you or it won't work. So there is really no such thing as truly kidnapping yourself. Just in case you were ever asked about that in a quiz or something.

Chiquita thought of one problem: what if there wasn't enough room for me in the back of the van? Indira thought of a second problem: that it might be very dirty in the back of the van – but that was only a problem for princess-type people and didn't apply to me.

'I don't mind getting dirty,' I said.

Indira looked as though I'd said I didn't mind eating dirt. But she made up for it by spying on Clive and Toby while they loaded the van to see if there was any room.

'There is room,' she reported back. 'And, even better, they cover a lot of their equipment in old sheets. So all you see is lumps. They might never spot that one of the lumps is actually Katie.'

Then she went off to wash her hands, as if just looking at the van had made her dirty.

We needed to find rope to tie me up with. That wasn't hard: Bernadette could 'borrow' some skipping ropes from Sister Vincent's gym store. Then we needed thick tape to gag me with. Indira was class monitor for tidying up the art room so she was allowed to be in there on her own and could most easily steal this vital kidnap equipment.

Now we needed the right moment. While Clive and Toby were packing up, Chiquita was going to create a diversion to allow enough time for me to climb into the back of the van, get tied up and hide under a sheet. She went to the classroom where Clive and Toby were in the middle of dismantling the lights and cameras at the end of the day. She was going to distract them by asking if she could have a go with the camera because she wanted to be a camerawoman one day.

She also had a plan B: 'If they refuse, I'll start screaming and crying for as long as possible. They'll have to stay with me until I've calmed down.'

Me and Bernadette watched Toby and Clive pack some lights into the back of the van. Then they went inside to fetch more things, leaving the rear door open. Hopefully, they would now be delayed by Chiquita. We crept towards the van, Indira keeping watch, and we climbed in.

We made our way to the very back. Bernadette tied my hands and feet, but loose enough so that I could untie myself and escape if needs be. The last thing was to put the tape over my mouth; this was the bit I wasn't looking forward to in case I suffocated. But as Bernadette pointed out, I could reach with my hands to pull the tape off if I couldn't breathe. And also I could breathe through my nose. So I would only suffocate if I was deliberately very stupid.

'Good luck,' Bernadette whispered as she covered me with an old sheet, clambered out of the van and scurried away.

I realized I was hungry. Too late to think about that now. But there's something to remember – if you're going to kidnap yourself, always have some snacks first. Still, if I looked a bit starved, that would probably make me seem more convincingly kidnapped.

As it was winter, it was already dark outside and even darker under the sheet. And, believe me, when I say winter, I mean cold too. I tried to keep curled up to be warm and also to take up as little space as possible. In some ways, I wanted to fall asleep so I could avoid feeling scared, but the metal floor was very uncomfortable. I also couldn't relax to fall asleep because I was nervous about Toby and Clive coming back to load the van. What if one of them thought, Hello, I don't remember this sheet, and found me before our plan had started?

I lay there like a sad ghost under my sheet, thinking how the girls would be going in to tea in the warm dining room, having hot drinks, bread and jam, whispering jokes to each other and giggling when they were told off for talking when they weren't supposed to.

I wished the school was in the town. At least then there would be traffic noise, people walking around outside. But it was in the countryside in the middle of nowhere. There were only spooky sounds to hear. The wind in the trees. Some far-off animal hooting – an owl maybe, rather than a slashing robot in armour imitating an owl . . . Better not to think about that . . . Oh, yes, and I could also hear the sound of my teeth chattering.

I never used to believe that people could be so cold their teeth would chatter cartoon-style, but mine were doing it, even though my lips were held together with tape. And the wind was really howling in the trees now. It felt like midnight even though it was only about four o'clock.

As well as thoughts of armoured robots, Bernadette's story about the execution floor and the cotton-wool stuffed heads of servants kept coming into my imagination but I chased it away, trying to think of nice things I could have had as pre-kidnap snacks if I'd thought of snacks . . .

But, and you will know this for a fact yourself, once you've had a frightening thought in the dark, even if you know it's not remotely true, your whole brain is jangled up and scared and there's nothing you can do until it's daylight.

Suddenly I heard men's voices. Clive and Toby were

complaining about the cold as they came towards the back of the van. As well as imaginary terrors, there was also the real fear of what Clive and Toby might do if they found me.

Somewhere between the school and the town there was a big lake. As I was so neatly tied and gagged, it would be very easy for them to just stop off and throw me into the water. Down, down I'd go, struggling to get free . . .

'I want a nice holiday somewhere hot when all this is over,' Clive said as he put something heavy into the van.

'Well, I expect you'll be able to afford it,' Toby said, also putting something heavy in the van. He sounded very sarcastic and Clive noticed.

'Yeah, all right,' he said crossly. 'But remember when you're lying on a beach somewhere that I was the one who found out about Stella Diaz.'

'And I'm the one who did the deal,' Toby said.

This was great – already they were going to spill the beans and I'd find out what they were up to at any minute . . .

But no. Clive just said, 'Let's get the rest of the stuff and get out of this place.'

'I thought we'd never get rid of that Diaz girl. Didn't she drive you mad with all those questions about the camera?'

'Completely mad,' Clive agreed. 'I don't know why she thinks she'd be any use operating the camera. She's certainly useless in front of it.'

'Oh, I know,' Toby complained. 'They're all useless.

Trying to get that skinny ginger one to smile. Hopeless. At least my sis has some charm about her.'

Clive laughed. 'And that pasty-faced Cockney one, the way she keeps saying "and so on" drives me mad. "Here's where we have our meals and so on. Here's where we have music lessons and so on." If I hear her say that one more time . . .'

Clive was imitating me talking in a really horrible way. I wished the sun tattoo on his neck would turn into a real sun and burn him up.

'At least she speaks,' Toby said. 'Not like that Diaz kid who only seems to know "yes" and "no".'

Clive replied, 'Well, the sooner I see the last of those brats—' And they walked away from the van again.

I hated them so much. They'd told us we were great all the time we were filming and now they were being completely rude about us. I hoped they'd go to jail for life for whatever they'd done. And so on.

I waited, now feeling upset as well as hungry, cold and nervous. They came back. Put more stuff in the van.

'Is that everything?' Toby asked.

'That's it,' Clive replied, and they banged the van doors shut, not noticing me under my ghost sheet. Idiots.

The van moved off. It felt as if I was being thumped around against the metal floor by every pebble in the road. After a while I started to feel a bit sick. I wriggled and lurched myself into a sitting position. I still felt sick.

And panicky. I took the tape off my mouth, which hurt like taking off a plaster. I thought it would help to get more air, but it didn't really.

We drove for what seemed like hours. I was freezing cold now, but at least feeling slightly car sick made me feel less hungry.

Finally we parked. I heard the front doors slam shut and I was alone.

All I had to do was wait long enough for the nuns back at the school to discover I was gone and call the police. Then I realized I had another thing to do: I had to not start thinking about wanting to go to the toilet.

Why is it that in detective books and films, when the detective is waiting hours for things to happen, he never says, 'But I didn't know what I was going to do about having a wee'? Sorry to mention such matters but in my opinion it is a big fault with most detective books and programmes.

CHAPTER TWENTY-SIX

Sometimes I could hear cars outside, doors slamming. I realized one big thing that was wrong with our plan, apart from the no-toilet problem, was that I had no idea what was going on back at school. So I didn't know if the nuns had noticed I'd been kidnapped yet. The plan would be ruined if I got out of the van too soon.

Of course, I found out later that what was actually happening was this: Bernadette, Chiquita and Indira were a bit scared that I'd be caught and murdered, so as soon as tea was over, they started wandering around the hall and classroom saying, 'I don't know where she is. Do you think she's ill and gone to bed? Do you think she's run away?'

Until finally Sister Ita heard them and asked, 'Who are you looking for?'

'Katie,' Bernadette told her. 'Didn't you notice she wasn't at tea?'

Sister Ita frowned. 'Now I come to think of it, I don't

remember seeing her at tea but I thought she was just, I don't know, around somewhere.'

Bernadette made a panicked face. 'Oh no, Sister, where has she got to? What if she's run away?'

Chiquita and Indira also tried to make very worried, scared faces.

'You're her friends,' Sister Ita said. 'Do you think she's run away?'

'That's what's strange,' Bernadette said. 'I'm sure she'd have said something to me if she was going to.'

Sister Ita frowned, crinkling up her red face so it looked like squashed tomato skin. 'We should tell Sister Vincent immediately. In the meantime, get the rest of your class and search the school and the grounds.'

Bernadette bossily got the class together and made them search. Danielle complained a lot, saying that she didn't care where I was but she knew the search was on the orders of the nuns so she had to do it.

When it was time for study, Sister Vincent called the whole school into the hall and asked if anyone had seen me. When there was no answer, she said she would be calling the police. Indira put her hand up and asked if Sister Vincent thought I'd been kidnapped.

Sister Vincent said: 'Good heavens, no, child. I suspect she's run off on some silly adventure but she must be stopped as it's cold and dark and anything could happen.'

But Indira had started the idea of kidnapping in

everyone's heads, which was our plan. By morning, with help from Chiquita and Bernadette, she would have got everyone worked up into a 'Katie's been kidnapped' frenzy. And in the morning, Clive and Toby would open the van and find me there tied up. I'd say, 'Everyone thinks I've been kidnapped, stop what you're up to or I'll say it was you who kidnapped me. If you confess and stop what you're doing, I'll just go back to school and say unknown strangers kidnapped me.'

I think you'll agree, this was an excellent plan. Except I hadn't thought about the toilet angle.

I could undo the skipping rope around my wrists quite easily with my teeth. Then I undid my feet. I could see through the windows that there were some bushes behind the van.

I would creep out, run into the bushes to solve the toilet problem, then get back in the van and tie myself up again.

There was too much clutter and equipment to climb over to reach the back doors. I crawled over the seats into the front. It was a still bit awkward, with lots of gear sticks and things prodding into me. Then I opened the door and jumped out. Carefully, I left the door slightly open and fled into the bushes.

When my problem was solved, I darted back to the van. I was in a hurry because the bushes had been a bit spooky and I knew I'd feel safer once I'd tied myself up in the van again.

I was in such a hurry I didn't notice that someone else was also heading towards the van.

I opened the passenger door wide enough to get in just as I heard a voice shouting, 'Oi! Who's that?'

I quickly tried to scramble over the seats into the back but someone grabbed me by the ankle. It was Clive.

'Get off!' I kicked at him.

But he opened the door wide, grabbed my kicking legs and said, 'Stop that!'

Then he stepped back, out of kicking range, and said furiously, 'Stop kicking me!'

I could see that there wasn't much point in trying to climb into the back of the van now. What I needed to do was get out and run away. I started wriggling backwards towards the driver's door but Clive jumped forward again and grabbed my feet. This time he had strong grip on them so I couldn't get a good kicking action going.

'Stop wriggling – you can't get away.'

'You'll be sorry. I know what you're up to!' I shouted, hoping someone in the hotel might hear me and rescue me.

Clive shook his head. 'You're such weird kids. And never mind what we're up to, what are you up to in our van?'

'None of your business,' I said. Childish, but it was all I could think of for the time being.

'It is my business. This is our van, full of very expensive equipment. You want me to call the police and say you're a thief?'

I was shaking, mostly from the cold but a bit from fright. I didn't want him to see that, so I folded my arms to keep still and to look tough.

'You could call the police,' I said. 'But then the nuns all think you kidnapped me.'

'What?'

'They think I've been kidnapped. They don't know to blame you yet but I'll say it was you if you don't tell me what you and Toby are really up to and stop doing it.'

'What if I just tell the nuns you hid in the back of our van and caused trouble? Don't the nuns think you're a bit of a troublemaker already?'

'No. No, they don't,' I lied. 'And kidnapping a child is very serious. You could be in jail by tomorrow.'

He laughed. 'Yeah, right.'

He let go of me, reached past me and picked up his mobile phone from the side pocket of the door. He pressed a speed-dial number.

'Yeah, Toby, I found my mobile. And something else. You better come out to the van.' Then he looked at me in a slightly threatening way. 'Nobody is up to anything, understand?'

'I know you are,' I said. 'And you'd better confess or you'll be in jail for kidnapping.'

He smiled and dialled another number.

'Hello? Is that Sister Vincent? It's Clive here. I think you might be worried one of your students is missing? Well, it seems she's stowed away in the back of our van.' He paused, smiling at me in a horrible way. 'No, I've no idea why she did it. But we'll bring her straight back. No problem, Sister.'

He gave me a 'so there' look as Toby came out.

Clive explained to Toby that I was going to pretend to be kidnapped if they didn't tell me what they were up to.

'But we're not up to anything,' Toby said, with the totally innocent smile that Danielle could do.

'I'll take her back to the school,' Clive said.

'OK,' Toby replied. Then he looked at me, pretending to be all hurt. 'I don't understand what's the matter with you. We've been nice to you, put you in the film ... Why are you making up stories about us?'

'It's not stories,' I said crossly.

'Well, I've got a lot to do – I haven't got time for this,' Toby said, and walked off back towards the hotel.

Clive looked annoyed. 'Nor have I,' he muttered. 'Come on then, sit straight, seat belt on.' Once I was in, he slammed the passenger door shut.

I couldn't believe that I'd tried to trap them with my fake kidnapping plan and now I was being told to put on my seat belt like a kid.

Too late, I realized that what I hadn't accounted for in my plan is that grown-ups, even weird ones like nuns, believe other grown-ups before they'll believe a kid. Clive was obviously counting on this. He knew Sister Vincent wouldn't listen to me unless I was actually injured or something.

I thought about jumping from the moving van to get actually injured but then realized that, even for me, that would be insane.

For most of the drive Clive said nothing, then he asked me, 'Why does it bother you if we're up to something?'

What a stupid question. 'What if you were really going to kidnap someone?'

He laughed then and said, 'Even Toby's not that bad.'

'But he *is* bad?'

Clive shook his head. 'If we're up to something, it's nothing like you think. It won't do anyone any harm.'

'So there *is* something.'

'What a nosy kid. Look, I'm telling you, there's no reason to get worried.'

'I don't believe you,' I said.

'Suit yourself.' Clive sighed and drove on faster towards the school.

CHAPTER TWENTY-SEVEN

Sister Vincent was waiting at the front door.

'Well, I have to say I am at my wits' end with you, child,' she said. 'The very end shreds of my wits.'

Then she stood to one side to let Clive bring me through to the hall. Although I was going to be in trouble, I was glad to be back in the warm.

'I can't apologize enough,' Sister Vincent said to Clive.

He smiled as if he was the nicest person in the universe, and said, 'Gave me a bit of a fright when I found her hiding in the van. I can't get much sense out of her – I suppose she wanted to run away.'

I'd had enough of this nicey, nicey talk and interrupted. 'No, Sister, that's not true. I was kidnapped.'

Clive just laughed and said, 'I don't know, Sister, she keeps saying that. It seems to be the story she's invented to cover up her antics.'

And I could see Sister Vincent believed him.

'Well, I'm sorry you had your time wasted with it all and thank you for bringing her back.'

Clive said, 'No trouble, Sister,' and had the cheek to grin at me and say, 'Behave yourself now.' Then he went off into the night, hands in his pockets to show how cheerful and carefree he was.

Now I tried telling Sister Vincent the real truth. The story rushed out of my mouth – how I'd pretended to be kidnapped so I could find out what crime they were planning. I told her about Clive saying there *was* something going on, even though he claimed no one would get hurt, but why should we believe——?

Before I'd even noticed her hands move, Sister Vincent had her whistle in her mouth and was blowing on it frantically.

In the deserted hallway the sound of the whistle was very loud.

Finally she took it out of her mouth. The sound still seemed to be filling the air.

'Now, child, do you know what the whistle means?'

'That you aren't listening?'

'No. It means stop. Stop, I can't bear any more of this nonsense. Do you realize we've been searching the school for you, and all your friends have been terribly worried?'

That was a relief – she didn't think the others were involved.

'Sorry, Sister,' I said.

'No, no, sorry won't do. I think enough is enough. When your mother and lovely grandfather come to the Christmas concert, I will have a meeting with them and we'll decide whether you should stay on at this school or not.'

There wasn't much I could say to that.

I went upstairs, quite glad I was being sent for a bath and bed. That seemed very cosy after the freezing van.

As for my disastrous-looking future – I could only hope that Toby and Clive were caught at their crime before Christmas.

Or maybe, out of shame, I would have to run away for real.

CHAPTER TWENTY-EIGHT

I had a bit of an argument with Bernadette, Chiquita and Indira, who all sat on my bed and started saying that they'd never thought the fake kidnapping plan was any good. Although they were pleased that I hadn't got them into trouble.

Bernadette even said, 'We've been in so much trouble lately and it's all because of you and your wild ideas.'

Wild ideas? How could she say such a thing to me? 'Bernadette, you know Clive and Toby are criminals.'

'I don't know,' she said, scowling at me.

'Perhaps we have bitten off more than we can chew' – Indira sighed – 'and we should perhaps leave matters to the authorities.'

'I'm bored with the whole thing now anyway,' Chiquita moaned. 'Let's just forget about it.'

I felt tired, stupid and as if I'd no real friends left in a crisis. I told everyone to go away and let me sleep. They did, too quickly. It seemed like they were glad of an excuse not to talk to me any more.

The next day, to make matters worse, Danielle came into the classroom and said, 'Oh, are you here, Katie? Not been kidnapped by your imaginary enemies?'

Lots of people laughed. I don't think my friends laughed.

I tried to ignore her.

'Hello? Earth to Katie? Or are you so used to everything being imaginary you don't know when real people are talking to you?'

Some more people laughed. Not my friends, I'm pretty sure.

'I expect they've only put you in the documentary because it's so funny to see someone so crazy.' Danielle laughed. 'Crazy Katie and her imaginary kidnappers.'

A bit like a crazy person, I lost it and grabbed a book off my desk and threw it. *David Copperfield*. He flew across the room and hit a vase of flowers on top of a high bookcase by the teacher's desk. While all this was happening to *David Copperfield*, I was shouting, 'Shut up, Danielle! It's you that's crazy, completely nuts!'

The vase flew off the bookcase, hit the side of the classroom door and broke, spraying water and blue flowers everywhere – just as Sister Vincent came through the door. Typical of my luck, I think you'll agree.

Danielle smiled at me like a grotesque grinning snake and slithered to sit innocently behind her desk.

Sister Vincent looked at the mess on the floor: water, flowers and *David Copperfield*. Then she glared around the room.

'Who threw that?'

I put up my hand – there was no point doing anything else. Then, to my surprise, Bernadette put her hand up too.

'Both of you. How could that be?' Sister Vincent looked very annoyed.

'I told her to throw it,' Bernadette lied.

'Well, she still shouldn't have thrown it,' Sister Vincent said. Then she rolled her eyes upward. 'Heaven forgive me but I've had enough. That's it. As you know, all the school sing the school song at the end of the Christmas concert. But not you two tiresome, silly little girls. You will not be present at the concert at all. You will be in here in the class-room in disgrace. The only girls in the recent history of the school to be completely banned from this event. In fact, in the whole history of the school. Now, everyone else come to the hall to practise the song. You two stay here and tidy up this horrifying mess, then sit and contemplate your end-less naughtiness and how naughty it is.'

Everyone filed out after Sister Vincent. Chiquita and Indira smiled at us sympathetically. Danielle whispered, 'Crazy Katie, Bonkers Bernadette.'

We both made faces at her but she pranced out of the

classroom, smiling as if she enjoyed having faces made at her.

I asked Bernadette why she had been so insane as to say she'd told me to throw the book.

'I just felt bad that you were in trouble all on your own.'

'Thanks,' I said.

Bernadette shrugged. 'Anyway, who cares about the concert? My parents will be in Hong Kong.'

'I expect mine will be trying to not have me expelled,' I said. 'So they won't care about the concert much.' Then I added, 'Not my parents, I mean, my mum and my grandad.'

Bernadette nodded understandingly, but I suddenly felt totally fed up with having to add that bit about meaning my grandad when I said 'my parents'. Never once in my life had I been able to say 'my parents' and mean just that.

I had a feeling the nuns would get rid of me no matter how much Mum and Grandad pleaded. So I'd be in disgrace all Christmas and it would be rubbish at home. I wished I was going to Hong Kong or somewhere exciting. Chiquita was going to New York with her mum. Indira was going to be in her parents' posh house in London. I'd be in disgrace in a little council house.

'Look out!' Bernadette said suddenly, disturbing my moany thoughts.

Toby and Clive were getting out of the van. They started unloading some equipment. We both got down on the floor because we didn't want them to see us.

'Don't worry,' Bernadette said. 'We've still got time to catch them.'

'Maybe,' I said. But I didn't really believe in my abilities with crimes any more.

We crawled around the classroom floor tidying up the pieces of broken vase and putting them in the bin. This meant we were under the teacher's desk when Toby and Clive came in.

'I think this is the best place, you see – clear view of the car park and then quickly out of the side door to grab her,' Clive said.

'Yes,' Toby agreed. 'I guess they can hide in here – everyone else will be in the hall. I'll let them know.'

They went out and Bernadette squeezed my arm.

'Kidnapping!' she whispered. 'You were right!'

But who were they going to grab? Indira? Chiquita?

We were so glad about our punishment now. We were going to be in the classroom that would also be the kidnappers' hideout.

We would solve the crime, save the day . . . and so on!

CHAPTER TWENTY-NINE

Next, nothing much happened for days and days. School went on: sometimes we were in the kitchen; sometimes we shouted insults at Danielle; sometimes me and Bernadette hung around the classroom while everyone else practised for the concert. The more I thought about how disgraced I was and how many plans had gone wrong, the more I completely lost confidence that I'd manage to finally do something successful and save the day.

I had a letter from Mum saying how much she was looking forward to Christmas and the Christmas concert ... Oh dear. She'd be so upset and ashamed to find out I was banned.

Then I had a letter from Grandad saying he was really looking forward to Christmas, although he was a bit sad he'd have to go away straight after New Year to help Stella with security at some charity events she had coming up in America. This made me more than a bit sad, as you can imagine.

Some days there was snow; some days we had Christmassy things like mince pies. Sometimes I wished I was someone else who didn't always get into trouble and wasn't going to be in deep trouble for Christmas.

Sister Vincent hardly spoke to me and Bernadette. She just looked at us as if she was thinking 'fiends' every time she saw us. Then, surprisingly, the morning of the concert, she gave us a pile of books to read while the concert was happening.

Bernadette said this was because she was starting to feel sorry for us. Then we looked at the books and they were all about the lives of holy saints. People she wanted us to copy, I expect, so we would stop being fiends.

Ages before the concert, Sister Vincent put us in the classroom and said, 'Now stay here quietly until you're called for. Then she drew the blinds on all the windows, saying, 'I don't think people should see that you're in here. You're not fit to be seen. And I don't want you waving out, understand?'

We nodded.

'Just sit quietly,' she said, and went out, closing the door behind her.

As soon as she'd gone, Bernadette jumped up and switched off the light. This was our plan: to hide under the teacher's desk in the dark until the kidnappers came in.

We were a bit squashed up, although it was much better

than being cold and lonely in the back of the van. Outside we could hear cars arriving. I expected Mum's bashed old car was there among all the fancy cars that most people's parents had.

Suddenly we stopped hearing cars and guessed everyone had gone into the school hall. Then we heard footsteps and whispering outside the classroom. The door opened; a torch shone in.

A woman said: 'This must be it.'

They moved around a bit. They must have been peering out through the blinds.

'Which is her car?' the woman asked.

'The big silver one there,' the man said.

Bernadette pinched me. I nearly squeaked but I knew what it was. 'She' in the silver car could only be Stella Diaz.

They weren't going to kidnap one of us, they were after Chiquita's mum!

There was a scraping noise as they sat down on chairs.

'How much longer?' the man asked.

'About half an hour,' the woman said.

Then they went quiet. Me and Bernadette hardly dared breathe. If they found us, who knew what they'd do?

After a while I heard a clicking sound – some kind of mechanism turning. I pinched Bernadette this time. The thing was, the noise . . . it sounded like it could be a gun. I knew guns very well from television detective programmes. They made that sound when you were loading them.

After what seemed like years there was a scrape of a chair.

'They're coming out,' the woman said.

'Right,' the man replied.

He followed the woman out of the classroom. The door shut softly behind them.

'Did you hear that noise?' I whispered. 'I've heard it on telly. It's a gun.'

Bernadette seemed to glow in the dark she was so amazed. 'A gun? What do we do now?'

'Follow them and start shouting a warning when we see Stella.'

'But if they've got a gun...' Bernadette panicked. Although it was a good reason to panic.

'OK, you run and phone the police from the pay phone. I'll shout at Stella to get down.'

We went very carefully along the corridor outside the classroom. We could see the man and woman at the end of the corridor to the right. They were standing on the porch, just inside the side door, with their backs to us. I pointed towards the phones in the opposite direction. Bernadette nodded and ran off. I hurried towards the side door and flattened myself against the wall, hoping the criminals wouldn't turn round. And hoping that if they did, it would be too dark to see me.

By the dim light of the porch I watched them. The man was pushing the door open. If I moved really quickly, maybe they wouldn't see me go out behind them.

I crept closer. I felt terrified. What if I was shot? How much would it hurt?

'There she is,' the woman said. I could see her arms moving. She must be getting the gun ready. I had to do it. I had to save Stella. Then I had the thought that really made me brave. As the bodyguard, Grandad might throw himself in front of Stella. It could be Grandad that was shot. I'd have to warn everyone – I'd have to leap on the woman.

I saw lights flashing and heard shouts. I thought I must be already shot. Then I realized I didn't feel shot, however that felt. I looked at the woman. She was walking forward with a camera in her hands and it was flashing. She had been making clicking sounds with a big camera, not a gun. This was still not a good thing. The camera woman could be distracting everyone with her blinding light while accomplices – that means some other people – grabbed Stella. The accomplices might have guns . . .

I yanked the door open and ran out past them, shouting, 'Stella, Grandad, run!'

I ran with my head down, in case of shots, so I almost knocked Stella over. Grandad was there, grabbing hold of me.

'Katie, what the——?'

I turned round to point at the danger.

The woman with the camera was shouting, 'Stella, Stella!' and the camera flashed again.

Grandad moved me to one side and left me. He ran at the woman and grabbed the camera. 'This is private!' he yelled.

The man ran past him and towards Stella, shouting, 'Stella, tell us about your secret daughter!'

To help Grandad, I ran and jumped on the man's back, pulling his hair.

He screamed. He turned round and round trying to push me off him. It occurred to me that he might not deserve to have his hair pulled so hard. After all, there didn't seem to be any gun.

Grandad let go of the woman but took her camera with him. He grabbed me by the waist and lifted me off the screaming man.

'Well done, love, leave it now,' he said. I think he was laughing.

He carried me over to where my mum was standing with Stella, Chiquita and Sister Vincent.

'What is going on?' Sister Vincent bellowed.

'Katie?' My mum grabbed me.

'It's journalists,' Grandad said angrily.

He was swinging the big camera around by its strap. It had all kinds of switches and attachments, things that might make a clicking noise . . .

'Oh, how did they get in here?' Stella tutted.

My mum was asking me if I was all right. I did seem to be. But I felt very shaky, as if I might faint. Next time I'd know that thinking you might be shot did make your knees feel wobbly afterwards.

Mum was asking me something else but I couldn't hear her. All I could hear was Sister Vincent.

'What did I say? What did I say?' she was bellowing.

We all looked at her. She was standing, hands on hips, looking like a fire-breathing dragon in a nun's veil.

'Katie!' she roared in my direction. 'You must remember what I said.'

I shook my head – I had no idea what she was on about.

'Come along, Katie, I think you're just the girl I need to help me. I promised Miss Diaz to take the fire hose to any reporters who turned up here uninvited. I always keep my promises. I believe you know where the hose is.'

The journalists were standing around saying things like, 'Come on, Stella, be reasonable . . . Just a few questions . . . Tell him to give us the camera back . . .'

I ran to get the hose, shouting for Chiquita to follow as I'd need someone to turn on the water.

I hauled the hose out of the shed, up to the car park and handed it to Sister Vincent, shouting, '*On!*' to Chiquita.

Sister Vincent shouted, 'Out of the way, Mr Milne!' to Grandad, who was trying to shield Stella from the journalists, standing with his arms out, saying, 'No! No questions!'

He moved to one side just as a huge jet of water spurted out and drenched the woman journalist.

Sister Vincent laughed like a maniac. 'Oh, tremendous fun!'

Then she turned the hose on the man, who was standing around, a bit confused, rubbing his hair. He screamed even more than from the hair-pulling when he was squirted.

Once they were both completely drenched, Sister Vincent threw the hose away onto the lawn and roared, 'Now do you frightful people understand that this is a private event on private property?'

The woman looked like an angry drowned cat.

'All right, we're going. But tell Toby Kirkham-Byles we'll want our money back.'

Sister Vincent asked them what they meant by that.

'He sold us a story about Stella's secret daughter, exclusive, before the reality-TV show comes out and everyone else knows. We gave him forty thousand pounds for exclusive access and a sneak preview of the documentary.'

'He had no right to give you access to my school,' Sister Vincent said. 'Now get in your car and go away immediately before I have you arrested.'

The journalists didn't need telling twice. They took the camera from Grandad, who had taken out the memory card, and ran squelching wet to their car. The sound of distant police sirens was coming closer. Bernadette had done her job.

'Dear, oh dear,' Grandad said to Stella, 'I told you you'd

need a second bodyguard even at a private event like this.'

'I had loads of bodyguards.' Stella laughed. 'I had Katie and Sister Vincent.'

'I can't apologize enough,' Sister Vincent said.

Stella laughed again. 'You said you'd put the hose on them and you did. What's to apologize for?'

'It *was* rather enjoyable.' Sister Vincent beamed.

Then she realized the hose was flopping around on the lawn, making muddy pools. 'Katie, dear,' she said. 'Do tell Chiquita she can turn off the water and come out of the fire shed now. Crisis averted and all that.'

But I didn't want to go because I needed to explain things to my mum, who was standing around looking very confused. I was going to start telling her about Toby and Clive but she asked the wrong question.

'What's going on, Katie? I didn't see you in the concert at all.'

I couldn't bear to tell her the truth but I'd have to.

'Oh, such an unfortunate thing.' Sister Vincent's big voice boomed over me as I started to mutter out an answer. 'Katie had a dreadful headache at the last minute. But luckily she recovered in time to save the day.'

I stared at her. She was a nun and she'd just told a big fat lie. Sister Vincent gave me a big smile and started moving away. 'You'll have to excuse me. I think I need to have a word with young Toby. As you warned me, Katie, he was always up to no good. Such a shock, such a good family.'

Chiquita came round the corner. 'I turned the water off,' she said, a bit pointlessly because we could see it was off.

'Good girl, good girl,' Sister Vincent said cheerfully. 'I must go. Katie, take your party to the kitchen to warm up and get tea and keep them away from prying eyes...'

The car park was now full of other parents, all looking curiously at Stella Diaz.

'This way,' I said, holding my mum's hand.

As we went round the corner, we bumped into Danielle and her very fancy-looking parents.

'Oh, I remember you,' Stella said to Danielle.

Stella shook hands with Danielle's parents politely, then said to Danielle, 'A shame your brother has rather spoiled the documentary for everyone.'

She walked on, leaving Danielle saying, 'What?'

And Danielle's mother saying, 'Don't say "what" like that to people, Danielle, it's very common...'

And her dad asking, 'Why is she saying Toby spoiled the documentary?'

So it sounded like there'd be lots of trouble at home for Danielle and Toby. Hah!

By the way, her parents looked very grand but they didn't have any axes or anything.

Next we bumped into Indira and her parents. Her mother was very beautiful and her father was friendly and fat. More introductions went on. While all the parents talked about how good Indira had been in the concert, I whispered to her what had happened.

'Squirted with the hose!' she squealed delightedly.

'Who was squirted?' her father asked.

'Oh, it's very complicated, Father,' Indira said. 'I'll explain in the car.'

Then she gave me a big hug. 'Happy Christmas, Katie. Well done.'

'Well done for what?' my mum wanted to know.

'Oh, just... Anyway, we have to go this way to the kitchen.'

In some ways I was disappointed that I wasn't going to see Clive and Toby get told off for what they'd done. Still, the kitchen table was full of cakes and biscuits. Bernadette was already sitting there with a big plateful.

'Sister Vincent told me to come in here,' she said. 'It's for the nuns' Christmas party but we can all have some.'

Sister Finton and Sister Legori were clucking around happily with tinsel attached to their veils. I thought it would have been even more Christmassy if they'd put glitter in their beards, but they hadn't.

'Oh, yes, apparently there's been a bit of excitement, dears, has there?' said Sister Legori.

'A bit,' I said.

'Well, you're all very welcome. Sit down – there are plenty of cakes and biscuits. Sister Patricia went panic-buying mad in the shops today – all we've had to do is put it out on plates.'

'A shame in some ways,' Sister Finton said. 'Last year we baked everything ourselves.'

So I could understand why Sister Patricia had gone panic-buying mad in the shops this year. So there wasn't a Christmas party of beard-bit grey cakes.

Everyone sat down in the warm kitchen. The little nuns poured tea for the adults and lemonade for us. They made an extra-special giggling fuss of Grandad.

It was a strange tea party – a supermodel, nuns, schoolgirls, Grandad and my mum. She looked lovely. She was wearing a suit that must have been new and her hair was cut shorter than I remembered.

After she'd had a few sips of tea she said, 'Can someone just go over it all again? What happened?'

But she didn't get her explanation because the door opened and George came in carrying Taratoo.

'The vet gave her the jabs while he was up at the farm,' he said. 'And she was as good as gold.' He put Taratoo in her basket. Then looked a bit embarrassed to see a great crowd of people in the kitchen.

I couldn't believe he'd just walked in. 'George?' I gasped. 'I thought you were in Spain.'

'I had to come back and help my brother. He broke his leg. Oh, of course, you know that – it was you who saved him. I haven't been around much, what with all the farm work. We had the vet up to see to a sick farm cat so I asked him to give the puppy his jabs—'

'Have some Christmas cake, George,' Sister Finton interrupted.

'And a cup of tea,' Sister Legori said.

'Well, I said I'd get back.' I could see George felt shy being surrounded by so many strangers.

The weird thing was that in all the excitement and hose squirting I'd completely forgotten about the whole George-being-my-dad thing. But then I realized my mum was staring at him. I thought she was staring because she didn't like seeing a dog in a kitchen but . . .

'George?' she said. 'Is that you?'

CHAPTER THIRTY

George looked bewildered.

'Do I know you?' He stared back at my mum but didn't seem to recognize her.

'George doesn't remember lots of things,' I said. 'He got hit on the head.'

'Katie,' Mum said, telling me off.

George smiled. 'No, she's right. There are lots of things and people from the past I don't know.'

'You don't know me?' My mum seemed really sad that he didn't know her. I had a weird feeling. I looked at Bernadette, who had stopped with a piece of cake halfway in her mouth. Was he my dad after all?

'I really don't remember things,' George said.

'How do you know him?' I asked Mum.

'We were friends,' she said. 'When I was just starting as a nurse, he was a really good friend to me when ... Well, when your dad ran off.'

I felt a pang of disappointment. Even though I'd only

been stupid about the dad thing and Grandad had sent me the photo of the blond man, I'd been hoping for something more.

George shook his head. 'I'm so sorry.' Then he looked at my mum and his expression changed. 'Yes, yes, I remember your face. That's who Katie reminded me of.'

'You were a student doctor. You found me crying in the supply cupboard at the hospital after my husband left and you were so kind to me.'

'Well, I'm glad,' George said. 'You seem like a very nice person.'

'So were you. Well, you still are. What happened? You're a farmer now?'

But there was no chance to hear George's life story. Sister Vincent came in with Toby and Clive.

'I've brought these two wretches in to apologize, Miss Diaz. It really is too bad what they've done.'

'Shall we not offer them cake then?' Sister Finton asked.

'Absolutely not, Sister,' Sister Vincent said.

Toby started spluttering. 'Miss Diaz, if I could just explain—'

Stella held her hand up to stop him talking. If she'd had a whistle like Sister Vincent, I think she'd have used that.

'I agreed to do an interview for the school's reality-TV show so I could explain what happened to me and Chiquita – how we were separated for years. I only agreed because the documentary was important to Chiquita. And I wanted to just explain the story once and get on with my life. Sister Vincent told you I wanted to protect Chiquita from press attention but you sold the story to one of the worst tabloid newspapers. Chiquita's a child, do you understand that? I want to protect her from that filth.'

'But the tabloids would have come up here after the documentary anyway,' Toby said in a smart-alecky way, obviously not a bit sorry really.

'And Sister Vincent would have chased them off. She certainly wouldn't have sold the story,' Stella snapped at him.

'Well, I don't think you're being very realistic.' Toby shrugged. 'The newspapers will always be following you around.'

'So that makes it OK to help them?' my mum snapped.

Clive just looked embarrassed but Toby looked annoyed.

'Well, I apologize, but I was going to give some of the money to charity.'

'Some of it,' Grandad scoffed.

'Anyway, enough of your lies,' Sister Vincent said. 'I will be telephoning the head of the television company so I expect that will be the end of documentary making for you two.'

'But we'll have to give the money back to the newspaper now,' Clive said. 'Please don't make us lose our jobs as well—'

'I don't understand,' I interrupted. Although I did

understand about Clive a bit, but why would Toby need to do all these bad things just for money? 'I thought the Kirkham-Byles were supposed to be massively rich.'

'That's right,' said Bernadette.

'Sometimes people are just greedy and don't know when enough is enough,' Stella said. 'Is that it, Toby, were you just being greedy?'

Toby looked sulky. 'My stupid parents are always giving money to charity and places like this school, so I don't get that much.'

'Well boo-hoo,' said my mum. 'You're an adult, you should earn your own money.'

'Quite right, quite right,' said Sister Vincent. 'And if your television company weren't making a donation to our hospital in India, I would tell them they couldn't show the documentary.'

'Look, I'm really sorry,' said Clive. 'I shouldn't have let myself get dragged into this business with the newspapers.'

'Liar,' Bernadette said. 'We heard you insisting on being involved – you weren't dragged.'

Clive glared at her, and the sun tattoo on his neck seemed to throb with rage.

'Yes, yes, well, too late now,' said Sister Vincent. 'Get out of here before I tell the police to arrest you for being spineless greedy fiends.' She shooed them out of the kitchen.

My mum shook her head. 'I knew this documentary was a bad idea.'

Stella smiled in agreement with her.

'Still,' said Bernadette, 'we'll get to be on television loads. And Katie Milk was right all along. There were crimes going on.'

'And now it's nearly Christmas,' said Chiquita, putting a huge biscuit in her mouth.

'Yes indeed,' said Sister Legori.

'Carol,' George suddenly said.

'Good idea!' squeaked Sister Finton. 'Let's sing a carol.'

'No, no,' said my mum. 'He's remembered my name.'

George was smiling at my mum. 'Yes. Your name is Carol.'

'That's right,' said Grandad.

'Oh, Katie, love,' my mum said, putting her arm round me. 'I know it seems strange, but when I was more miserable than I'd ever been in my life, George helped me keep things together, helped me keep calm at work and not lose my job.'

George looked embarrassed. 'I don't remember.'

'Doesn't matter,' said Grandad. 'You're all right by me.'

George smiled his nice smile.

Sister Finton still hadn't understood what was going on and started singing: '*O little town of Bethlehem . . .*'

So we all gave in and joined in to keep her happy.

CHAPTER THIRTY-ONE

When I got home I felt close to tears when I saw how beautifully decorated the house was. I realized my mum did this much decorating every year, even when she had hardly any money. The difference this year was the massive pile of presents, far more than I'd ever had before.

'It's your grandad. He's bought you presents from all over the world,' Mum said.

Grandad shrugged. 'Well, Stella's always shopping so I had to go with her.'

'But don't expect the same next year,' Mum said. 'Your grandad's going back to being his boring old self.'

Grandad shrugged again. 'It was all very exciting going around the world with a supermodel. But I've had a little chat with Stella. It's been great but I miss my quiet life. So I'll just do this last job after the New Year and then that's it. I want to get back to my little flat and have time to help your mum with her shopping.'

'You don't want an exciting life?' I asked.

'It's been very exciting,' he said. 'But I'd like a rest now.'

'Funny old thing,' Mum said, hugging him.

I was glad really. He'd be back in his little flat, watching crime programmes and reading detective books – the grandad I was used to. Without hair gel.

Mum showed me upstairs to my room, wanting me to see how she'd redecorated it with new wallpaper and everything.

'I thought I'd make it look a bit posh, what with you being a reality-TV star now.'

I knew how busy she was so it was amazing she'd had the time.

'You're so great, Mum.'

'No, you're great, and you've linked me up with George again. He's such a nice man. I'm going to write to him, telling him about all the chats he had with me to cheer me up. Maybe all those details will help him get his memory back.'

Grandad winked at me. 'Who knows, this could be the start of a big romance.'

'Don't be silly,' Mum snapped at him. 'He was just my friend when Katie's dad left and I want to help him now if I can.'

'I don't care about dads,' I said, and suddenly I meant it. 'A mum and a grandad is the best thing.'

Mum hugged me and said she'd missed me. Then she stepped back, looking at me for a long time, the way she did when she was after the complete truth. 'But I think you're having a good time at that weird school. Is that right? Are you happy there?'

I didn't know if I could honestly say I was happy, not all the time. But we'd got to be on television, we'd solved a sort of crime and saved a puppy. And as Bernadette said when I said goodbye to her, 'I'll bring you back something good from Hong Kong. And won't it be great next term? We'll have so much to torment Danielle with.'

'And we'll have been on telly on New Year's Day, so maybe people will try and kidnap us or some other adventures,' I suggested.

Chiquita had groaned. 'Can't we just be at school in a normal way next term, without loads of adventures and crimes?'

'Are you crazy?' Bernadette stared at her. 'That's the best bit.'

Chiquita sighed. 'Sometimes. I suppose.'

'Always,' I said. 'The adventures, crimes and so on are *always* the best bit.'